THE LAST HARD

In his mind he tried
of Zach Provo. It ha
and the image was
A man like that, ho
in twenty-eight year
the mouth, faded the
made the hard brown body flabby? Changed the tough, taut, commanding presence into flaccid weakness? It wasn't possible. Not Provo. A man like that, hardship wouldn't grind down; it would only polish him up, like hard steel against a grindstone.

But maybe that was just a hope. Maybe he wanted Provo to be faster and tougher than ever. To increase the challenge.

I'm going to nail him, Sam Burgade thought. *I hope they don't get him before I get a crack at him.*

Also by the same author, and available in Coronet Books:

The Threepersons Hunt
Tripwire
Death Wish

The Last Hard Men

previously titled GUNDOWN

Brian Garfield

writing as Frank Wynne

CORONET BOOKS
Hodder and Stoughton

To D.E.W. with Apologies to Parker

First published 1971 by Dell Publishing
Co. Inc., New York, as Gundown by Frank Wynne

Coronet Edition 1974
Second impression 1976

Printed and bound in Great Britain for
Coronet Books, Hodder and Stoughton, London
By Cox & Wyman Ltd, London, Reading and Fakenham

ISBN 0 340 18295 4

CHAPTER ONE

WHEN Provo tripped, on purpose, over his leg irons, he let loose of the sledgehammer and fell on his hands. He timed the fall to put the fist-sized rock under his chest. When he started getting up, the rock was enclosed in the circle of his fist.

Guard Harrison came wheeling back down the hill road along the line of shackled prisoners, hefting his riot gun like a club. His big face was angry-red, peeling under the Yuma sun. 'Shake it up, Provo.'

'Don't shit in your britches.'

Harrison's pale eyes studied him with hot mistrust. He turned to reach down and pick up Provo's discarded sledgehammer, and glanced up the hot dusty hill. The front of the line had gone across the top — Guard Johnson was up front somewhere.

Guard Harrison seemed to catch it coming, out of the corner of his eye, but he was too slow. Provo smashed the rock into the back of his head.

It stunned the guard. He went to his knees, eyes losing focus. Provo jumped at him, rolled him over on his back away from the riot gun. Harrison was too dazed to fight, but his eyes showed his distress; sweat burst out in beads on his upper lip.

George Weed said, 'Kick the shit out of him, Zach.'

Provo ignored it. He reached across Harrison to get the riot gun.

Guard Johnson came in sight on the hilltop, looking to see what had stopped the marching line. Provo levelled the riot gun. 'I'd stay friendly.'

But Johnson's gun muzzle lifted. Provo pulled the trigger: the buckshot blast ripped into Johnson's chest and exploded his heart. Spasm closed his hand around the trigger and his gun erupted into the ground; its recoil knocked it out of his fists.

Provo could tell Johnson was dead by the way he fell. He spun towards Harrison, worked the pump action of the riot gun, and braced himself. But Cesar Menendez was already on top of Harrison, dragging the next man after him on leg chains; Menendez had his thumbs against Harrison's eyes and his knee in Harrison's gut. Harrison tried to struggle — got his hands on Menendez's wrists. The little Mexican batted them away with contemptuous indifference and went for the throat, thumbs against larynx. It only took a few seconds.

Provo's fiery eyes shifted from face to face. 'They made a mistake, marching us this far out of Yuma to build their fucking road. Nobody near enough to remark those gunshots. We're out.'

Young Mike Shelby was dubious. 'We ain't likely to get far in these irons, Zach. The keys are back in the yard captain's office.'

Provo bounced the riot gun in his enclosed fist. He reached down with his free hand to pick up the sledgehammer. 'We've got these. Bust the chains, anyway — worry about the ankle cuffs later. Unless some of you want to walk back inside the walls?'

Provo smiled, and moved suddenly: he did most things suddenly. He lifted the hammer overhead in both hands and brought it down hard on the chain between his foot and Menendez's. It crumpled a link but didn't break it. A knotted muscle bunched at Provo's dark jaw line; he swung again, swung a third time, and parted the chain.

There wasn't much talk. Hammers started swinging all up the line, driven by biceps hardened on the Yuma rock pile.

Provo picked up the riot gun, sat down in the dirt, and splayed his legs out straight. The two-foot chain hung slack between his ankles. 'Bust me loose, Menendez — and you ricochet any pieces into my balls, I'll kick your ass into the middle of next week.'

Young Mike Shelby said, 'He's joshin' you, Cesar. He's too

old to have much use for them anymore. Anyhow he's been in Yuma so long he's forgot how.'

'Twenty-eight years,' Provo breathed: the Yuma gates had closed on him in 1885.

Menendez's hammer clanged off the chains; finally they broke. Provo stood up dragging the ragged ends. Menendez said, 'Cot it off with a hacksaw, if you can get near one. Only take about five hannerd strokes.'

'If he don't cut his ankles off instead,' Mike Shelby said. 'That'd be a lot quicker.' Shelby was always ready with a sour humorous remark. He only had six months behind him, they hadn't crushed it out of him yet.

Provo's dark hatchet face swivelled towards Menendez. 'Come on up the hill with me. Let's take that other gun away from Will Gant before he decides to walk off with it by himself.'

'Orrai,' Menendez agreed.

They walked up the hill past swinging hammers. Provo had his finger inside the trigger guard of the riot gun, the slide balanced across the crook of his elbow. Portugee Shiraz, vulpine faced, grinned through bad teeth and said, 'What you gonna do next, Zach? Part the waters?'

'You just stick with me, Portugee.' Provo went on up the line with Menendez.

Will Gant saw them coming. He swung his big-bellied shape around ponderously and thought about picking up Johnson's riot gun from the ground — he had put it down to use both hands on his sledge.

'Naw, Menendez said, 'I wouldn't think like that, Will, it ain't es-smart.'

Gant kept thinking about it, though — measuring the distance, judging the angle of Provo's gun muzzle. The heavy roll of his lips peeled back nervously. 'Yair,' he said, 'I guess not. You want the gun, hey, Zach?'

'I've already got a gun,' Provo said. 'Menendez wants the gun.'

Gant thought about that, visibly. Finally he said, 'You waitin' on me to fight you for it, Menendez?'

'Naw, you lazy turd. I ain't got time for such truck.'

'Then get yo' dumb ass on over here and pick it up. I ain't rightly fixin' to mess with you.'

'Smart,' Zach Provo commented. 'Go ahead, then, Menendez.'

Menendez, with a thin smile, bent down to pick up the gun. He kept his head cocked, kept his eyes on Will Gant looming above him. Gant didn't stir. Menendez hefted the riot gun and went over to the dead guard to strip the blood-darkened cartridge belt off him.

Provo was counting heads from his vantage point on top of the hill. Will Gant waddled over and ranged himself alongside him. 'You takin' over now, Zach?'

Twenty-seven men, Provo tallied. Too many: too unwieldy. Distracted, he said, 'What do *you* think?' And without waiting a reply, climbed the steep pitch alongside the road to the summit twenty feet higher. From here he could make out a little bit of the brown glint of the Colorado River, and the bluff where the ruins of Fort Yuma stood on the far side, in California. The flayed hilly landscape was empty of movement. The sun, on this early morning in July, was hard as brass. He had it behind him. He turned a slow circle on his heels, surveying the great desert baking pan eastward, the line of stunt trees along the Gila and distant arid mountains. He shaded his eyes with a hand, saw nothing — no stirrings, no dust — and skittered back down to the road.

The hammers were still ringing. He waited for them to finish. Menendez fixed himself to him, at his shoulder. 'What now?'

'We get rid of the sheep,' Provo said. His eyes were narrowed in a thoughtful squint.

'And keep the goats?'

'Aeah.'

Menendez picked at his scalp and studied his fingernail. 'Then you got a plan in mind.'

'Maybe I do,' Provo said. He filled his chest and bellowed 'All right, everybody up here!'

While they gathered slowly around him, Provo's eyes dreamily tracked a scorpion under the shade of the rock shelf on the slope beyond the road. Its tail stinger was curled up over its back. Portugee Shiraz and Lee Roy Tucker sat down in the road, hammers across their laps. The rest crowded around, stinking of sweat, staying on their feet, and there was a lot of excited talking until Provo yelled at them to quiet down.

'We've got to split this bunch up,' he said when he had their attention. 'We've got maybe three hours to get shet of this place before the noon water wagon comes. I want them to find tracks going every which direction. Alcorn and Pete Cruz, you take Torres and those two over there and walk north along the river till you get to Quartzsite.'

Tom Alcorn said, 'Jesus, that's eighty-five mile, Zach, we can't just — '

'You can — or maybe you'd rather end up back in the hole? You can walk it in two days, drink out of the river, keep out of sight if you hear anything, duck into the river if you hear dogs. You find yourselves a blacksmith shop in Quartzsite after dark sometime and get rid of those irons and then you're on your own.'

Lee Roy Tucker picked up the hammer in his lap. His adenoidal mouth was open; he was thin as a sapling, with pinched eyes and buck teeth. 'Who elected you to give awders, Zach?'

Provo's riot gun stirred. 'I won't waste time arguing. Alcorn, get your bunch moving. Now.'

'Shee-yit,' said Lee Roy Tucker, but he stayed put and watched Tom Alcorn and the other four walk away over the hill without remark. They were happy to go: Pete Cruz was talking about his woman in Guaymas when they walked out of earshot beyond the hilltop.

Provo singled out four more and sent them west, told them to wade across the Colorado and lose themselves in the California badlands. They didn't like the idea much but Provo had the gun, and they went. None of them promised to stick to the route he had dictated, but it didn't matter to Provo; all he wanted was to get rid of them.

He sent seven more, most of them Mexicans, due south — told them to hold to that course until they got well south of Yuma, across the Border into Mexico. Then they could walk east along the canals to Calexico. They grumbled, and went. Probably they'd get rounded up within twelve hours.

He sent the three old-timers down the Gila, eastward. The river was dry, only a few sinkholes, but they went, because Provo had the gun and Provo was a tough breed to tangle with; and because Cesar Menendez just stood there with his riot gun, watching them all with his fast little eyes.

Provo counted heads again. 'Nine of us. That'll do.'

'Do what?' young Mike Shelby asked. 'What you got in mind, anyway?' Shelby was the only one of them with balls enough to ask that kind of question against Provo's gun, but Shelby was the only one who knew how to take the sting off a challenge with an amiable smile. He had a wide friendly face and a head full of chestnut hair, and the innocence of his nineteen years.

Provo looked them over, walking around, going from face to face. 'This time tomorrow,' he said, finally, 'those others will all be back in Yuma if they're not dead. Same thing can happen to us if we don't work together. Everybody understand me?'

Lee Roy Tucker said, 'Maybe some of us might rather not take awders from you, Zach.'

Provo shifted the riot gun to his left hand. His right hand gripped Lee Roy's arm. Lee Roy burst out in a grey sweat. The steel fingers bit into his arm, the strong thumb casually working flesh against cartilage against bone. Provo said, 'When I say jump, Lee Roy, you say How high?'

He let go of Lee Roy's arm and stepped back. Lee Roy looked uphappy, as if his shorts were bunching up. 'I don't think I want to mess with you, Zach.'

'You bet your ass you don't.'

Anticipating trouble from Will Gant, Provo wheeled that

way. Gant was tugging at a thick black hair in his nostril. The blunt head was anchored on a thick neck that bulged with folds of fat; the eyes were crafty. Provo didn't bother to watch the eyes, with which Gant would be likely to feint; he watched Gant's feet instead. 'How about it, Will?'

'Depends what you got in mind.'

It was easy enough to read in Gant's sullen face: he'd sooner herd sheep than follow orders from a half-breed Navajo. But Provo had the gun. Provo said, 'I'm going to get us out.'

'All right. You won't have no trouble with me.' Gant relaxed; his feet shifted and splayed.

Provo turned away, satisfied. 'Everybody pay attention now. We're going to walk straight over to the Colorado and sink ourselves down in the arrow-weed over there until dark. Sweat it out. On the far side of the river, so the dogs won't get to us. Come dark, we wade downriver into Yuma.'

'*Into Yuma!*' Lee Roy Tucker yelled.

'Shut up and stay still. We wade into Yuma and we wait under the ferryboat dock until sometime after midnight. There's an eastbound S.P. freight comes in across the bridge about two in the morning. Pulls out for Tucson around three. There's always half a dozen zinc-lined meat-hanging icebox cars. We climb into one of them. They'll search all the cars on the train but we hid back in the corners behind the carcasses, underneath. They won't take much time to search — they can't hold an ice car open for long, everything'd melt. Middle of the night, they'll be tired out by then anyway. They won't find us as long as everybody keeps quiet. We're going to freeze our asses but we'll make it. Soon as the train pulls out of Yuma we pitch the ice out and get ourselves thawed out. We jump off when she slows down at some town up the line and we lay belly-flat in the scrub until she's gone by. Then we shanks-mare into town and saw off these irons after dark, and get horses under us.'

Mike Shelby said, 'You've got all worked out.'

'I've had twenty-eight years for it.' He looked them over with icy contempt. 'Everybody hear me the first time?'

Lee Roy's jaw was set. 'You got short brains, Zach. They bound to get aholt of us.'

'Like hell they are. Don't be a farmer.'

Lee Roy was rubbing his arm where Provo had squeezed it. Provo said, 'You can do this with your teeth or without them. Which way you want, Lee Roy?'

Lee Roy licked his upper lip. 'I don't know. Maybe I'd just as soon go it alone, you don't mind.'

'I mind,' Provo said, flat. 'Nobody busts loose now, Lee Roy. Not after you've heard the plan. We go in together and we stick together — like flies on flypaper.'

'Why? One less man, make it that much easier for you, Zach.'

'I can't have you wandering into a posse and yapping to the law what we're doing. Understand? Now you go ahead and walk away from here if you're still a mind to, Lee Roy. But it'll take you all the rest of your life to walk two steps. Hear?'

Lee Roy scuffed his feet and scowled and didn't argue.

With a tongue dipped in vitriol, Provo snapped at them all 'I was born a few minutes ahead of the rest of you fools — just remember that. Come on, Menendez.' He turned on his heel and walked west, towards the river. The loose ends of the chains whacked him around the ankles but he didn't slow down.

When he looked back the rest of them were following. Menendez, with the riot gun, was herding them.

It was stinking hot in the arrow-weed rushes. The late afternoon sun beat down on the muddy surface of the river. They could still hear the dogs baying, going away upriver on the far bank, probably tracking the Alcorn bunch on the trail to Quartzsite. He had planned it like that.

Menendez said, 'Sonoma bitch, it's gonna work.'

'We're not out yet.'

'Bot it's gonna work. *Seguro que sí.*' The cruel fox-thin face smiled. 'What's that song you humming?'

'Owl Song.'

'Hey?'

'They sing it on the Reservation in hard times,' Provo said. 'Owl's a tough bird.'

'You ain't a fullblood Navajo, are you?'

'Half,' Provo said.

'Me, I'm half Messican and half es-Spanish and half Yaqui and half Texano and half focking rattlesnake, I guess. Listen, Zach, what we gon do after we get horses?'

'I don't know about the rest of you. I know what I'm going to do.'

'Ahjess?'

'I want Sam Burgade,' Provo said. He slapped a mosquito. 'I want Sam Burgade's cocksucking hide on a spit.'

'Hell, ain't you got nawthing better'n that to aim for, Zach?'

Deep hate was a fervour that got stronger with time. Provo shook his head. 'I want him, Menendez. I want to peel the tough old bastard right down to a whimper.'

'Hell, he's got to be a real old man by now.'

Provo didn't say anything. After a while Menendez said, 'Sam Burgade ain't nawthing but a tired old man, Zach. You'll suit yourself, I guess, but it ain't es-smart, what you fixin' to do. You want to get your hands on Burgade, you gonna have to show your ef-face right in the middle of Tucson. Tucson's a big town. They got a lot of law there.'

Provo grunted.

Menendez said, 'And it ain't as if he was some old *mestizo* nobody cared nawthing about, Burgade, he's an important es-sonomabitch. Maybe he don't tote a badge no more but he's got a lot of important frands. They hang you sure.'

'If he's riding high that's fine,' Provo said. 'The ground will hit him a lot harder when he falls.'

'Shit, whatever he done must've been a focking long time ago, Zach.'

'Shut up,' Provo said.

They kept close to the bank, slipping and sucking in the mud, wading into Yuma under the wharves of the old river-boat shipyards. The crosshatched spindle tracery of the S.P.

railroad bridge was a latticed silhouette against the night sky. Lamplight reflected off the dappled surface of the Colorado. The water was warm, a fast current that kept them moving downstream. Provo had the riot gun over his shoulder to keep it dry.

The ferryboat was over on the California side. They gathered under the landing slip of the Arizona side and waited. Provo's flesh had already begun to pucker from waterlogging; he climbed up into the woodwork under the ferry dock to dry off. The others took perches in the framework around him, like pigeons resting.

A federal motorboat putted by, coming downstream fast on the current, it's electric search light sweeping the river. It didn't have a chance of picking them up where they hid. It went by and there was only the faint lapping of the river against pilings, the clatter of wagons and the occasional cough and sputter of a passing motorcar. Sometime around eleven, the westbound passenger flyer roared across the bridge towards San Diego. They had another three hours to wait.

Someone urinated into the river nearby — the trickle was plainly audible. The ferry came across on its guy ropes, gasoline engine chattering, carrying two horseless carriages and a horse-drawn victoria and a dozen pedestrian passengers. Provo took a strong grip on the piling and held on while the ferry rammed into the slip and made everything shake. It didn't knock anybody off. The ferry got rid of its load and a new California-bound load came aboard. Provo couldn't see it; he could hear it. Someone's boots tramped the dock heavily and he heard a hard voice talking to the boatman: 'Keep an eye on the river tonight, Charley — God knows maybe they'll try to come down on rafts or something.'

'How many of them convicts you boys got back?'

'Picked up three on the Gila and a half dozen Mexes down south of town. The Chief just telephoned in from Quartzsite, they got five or six pinned down in a ranch house halfway up there, holdin' out with the rancher's guns. We'll get 'em soon as they run out of cartridges. Last I heard the dogs picked up another bunch that went west acrosst the river.

Prob'ly round them up by sunup. Just a matter of time, Charley, just a matter of time. We'll get 'em all, just as sure as they's a hole in your ass.'

The boots tramped back to hard ground and the ferry chugged away. Menendez said in Provo's ear, 'I hope that essonomabitch is wrong, hey? They ain't gon get us now, are they, Zach?'

'Not me they ain't,' Provo murmured. 'Not until I make Sam Burgade sweat some blood, they ain't.'

It worked fine. A railroader opened the side door and flashed an electric torch around quickly and slammed the zinc door shut. Didn't glimpse them. They all sat in the thick dark and trembled with cold until the train started up with banging couplings and slowly picked up steam. Provo waited until he couldn't stand the cold any longer, and then he hummed the Owl Song to himself and waited another fifteen or twenty minutes, and when Menendez joined the chorus of groans in the dark Provo smiled, because no one could see his face, and said under his breath, 'Not half bad for a fifty-two-year-old half-breed,' and got up and shoved the sliding door open and said, 'You bastards start heaving that ice out of here before we all turn blue.'

The train started to slow down for Gila Bend about six in the morning. When it was half a mile out, Provo slid the right-hand door open and nodded to Menendez. Menendez jumped — landed running like a cat. Provo poked the rest of them out, fast, with his riot gun and went out last, after pulling the door as nearly shut as he could and still squeeze through. Maybe they wouldn't find the warm icebox car until Tucson or maybe even El Paso.

He hit easy on both feet, legs bent against the fall, went over on his shoulder and rolled. He didn't lose his grip on the riot gun. His shoulder was a little banged up and he'd bruised one heel, but that was all right. He bellied down in the brush and watched the long train clatter past. The caboose went by and he waited until it was into town beyond the outskirt labourers' shacks; then he spoke softly and gathered them around him and said, 'We make for the nearest shack up yonder. We get inside it and we wait for dark. Move.'

He let Menendez lead the way. He waited until they had all crawled past before he fell in at the back of the line. Broken chains rattled on their ankles. Provo hung back a little: better not to let any of them see he was favouring his right foot from the jump. They kept to a line of approach that interposed the cluster of shacks between them and the town. Nobody was likely to see them, but Menendez moved bent double and the rest followed, suit, dodging from greasewood bush to paloverde. Clump to clump.

Menendez stood up against the corner of the weather-blasted grey shack, eeled around the corner and disappeared. Provo tensed, squinting into the morning sun. But after a minute the back shutter flapped open and Menendez waved them in.

Provo came in last and pulled the warped door shut behind him. The nine men made a dense crowd in the little shack; it was barely big enough to accommodate two occupants. He could smell the sweat already, and the day hadn't started to warm up yet. Under the tar-paper roof it would get up to a hundred and twenty in here by mid-afternoon.

Young Mike Shelby said, 'Maybe we ought to split up some. Take a couple more cabins, three men in each one.'

'We stick together,' Provo said.

'Why?'

'I want you all where I can see you.'

Lee Roy Tucker said, 'For how long?'

'Until we get rid of these irons and get ourselves into clothes everybody won't recognise.'

'Sounds reasonable,' Mike Shelby said, and sat down on one of the two cots. There was a rickety table with a lamp and washbasin. Shelves nailed on one wall — a few boxes and cans of food. George Weed, black-skinned and full of disgust, slid his back down the wall in the front corner until he was sitting with his shoulders wedged in. 'I don't suppose anybody's got a deck of cawds.'

Provo studied them covertly, one at a time, measuring them. He took his time.

Menendez: little, fox-quick, cruel, practical. Mike Shelby: young, level-headed, good-humoured, a friendly face and a shaggy head of chestnut hair and big tough hands. Lee Roy Tucker slat-narrow, buck-toothed, a complainer, but Lee Roy had handled blasting caps, working in a quarry, and knew explosives. Portugee Shiraz: part Portuguese, part Negro, eighteen years into a thirty-year noncommutable sentence for having knifed his wife and two children, one of whom had died; Portugee had the snout of a mountain wolf and he loved knives, all kinds of knives, he had worked in a slaughterhouse. Will Gant a very big brute with a belly on him, not quite as slow in the head as he seemed. George Weed: black, square-built, his hair like a wire-wool skullcap, lazy eyes; contained and quiet except for occasional bursts of anger. Taco Riva: ex-mountain bandit, ex-vaquero; Taco loved horses, in all possible ways. Joaquim Quesada a big-nosed brute with thick shoulders and a deep chest, a grey-monks fringe around his bald head, his face purple with tiny broken blood vessels — an alcoholic, an incorrigible petty criminal, and in spite of his bulk, an expert sneak-burglar.

And the ninth man. Zach Provo. He didn't need to size up himself.

His attention went back to Cesar Menendez. Menendez had quick spidery hands and a cynical mouth. His face and hands were slightly fire-scarred: he had burned down the Santa Cruz County jail around him in a fit of rage, and been sentenced to six years for arson. In a way Menendez was the key. No one man could handle a squad this big by himself; a man had to sleep sometime. There had to be a second-in-command who could be depended on. Shelby might be dependable, as far as it went, but Shelby was too young and too easy-going to command their respect. The rest of them, prison dregs, were born followers. Or maybe loners. But not leaders. Menendez was the only leader, himself aside. He didn't know, or care, whether Menendez liked him; but he had the feeling Menendez respected him — not out of fear, but out of admiration for his brains.

Provo licked his upper lip, like a cat washing itself. It was worth a try, anyway. Menendez was over at the door, watching Gila Bend town through cracks in the splintered boards. The sun was hitting that face of the shack and the others had crowded away towards the cool side, of the room, squatting around in little knots of dulled talk. Provo moved casually to the door and spoke in a voice calculated to reach no farther than Menendez's ears:

'You willing to stick by me a while longer?'

'You asking or telling?'

'Asking.'

Menendez glaced at him out of the edge of his eyes. 'What you got in mind?'

'You'll see. Just back me.'

'I don't know, Zach. If it's about Sam Burgade — '

'What if it is?'

'I got nawthing against Sam Burgade. That's your fight, not mine.'

'What if it gets you a free ticket out from under the law?'

'How?'

'Just stick by me.'

Menendez thought it over. 'Orrai. For a while, anyhow. I'll es-stick aroun' until I see how it blows.'

'Sure. You never know, you might even get your hands on that cache of railroad money I buried twenty-eight years ago.'

'Hell, you prob'ly don' even remember where you put it, that long ago. I never believed moch in that rumour.'

'It came to pret' near forty-eight thousand dollars. In gold eagles. Two hundred pounds of gold. They got me but they never got the money back.'

'You making me an offer, Zach?'

'Maybe.'

'You better es-spell it out a little clearer, then.'

'This ain't the time. But you just keep it in mind.'

'Ahjess. I'll do that.'

Provo moved away into the centre of the shack. 'All right,' he said, and got their attention. 'Tonight Menendez goes into town for a hacksaw and some food and clothes. We'll get fixed up to look like civilians. After that you-all are figuring to steal horses, split up and run for it. That's all right for them as want it. I don't particularly recommend it. What chance you going to have, without a cent in your kick? You'll just get rounded up one at a time. Nothing to show for it but shrivelled guts and saddlesores and a few days running like hell through the brush.'

Mike Shelby said, 'You're talkin' like you got something better to offer.'

'I have. But maybe you people would rather let them surround you with telephone messages and posses out of every county seat from here to Oklahoma. Maybe you've had enough of my ideas.'

Shelby said what Provo knew he'd say. 'You done all right up to now, Zach. Let's hear what you got in mind.'

Provo glanced casually at Menendez, met a glance of bland unconcern, and squatted on his haunches. 'We're going to get ourselves a healthy stake and take care of some personal business and then we're going to head for a hideout where the law can't touch us. All of us. We stick together all the way through, just like we've stuck together up to now. How about it?'

They exchanged glances among themselves. Lee Roy scowled at him but didn't say anything. Finally Mike Shelby said, 'Go ahead, Zach.'

'In a minute. What I've got in mind, it's going to take timing and planning. It'll take all of us to bring it off. But it's just like getting out of Yuma — I can't have any of you people hearing me out and then deciding you don't want to do it. Nobody cuts out on me. Anybody wants to leave, say so right now, and we'll wait till after dark when he's gone to talk about the rest of it. How about it? Anybody want to call it quits?'

He looked around, without expression. Implying if anybody wanted to quit, there'd be no hard feelings. It was a lie: if anybody tried to back out, Provo would kill him. But there wasn't much point in saying so.

'Lee Roy?'

'I don't rightly know. I don't hanker to ride out alone and git my ass blowed off. I don't rightly know this country arand here. How long this binness take?'

'Three, four days. A week maybe.'

'We split up after that?'

'After that,' Provo said, 'I don't give a shit what you do, Lee Roy. But whatever it is, at least you'll have a stake to do it on.'

'How big of a stake?'

'A few thousand, at the least.'

Will Gant said, 'Seems to me that's worth thanking about.'

Lee Roy said, 'I expect I'll go along, Zach.' His tone said he didn't like it much but he liked the alternatives even less. That was all right; Provo didn't care about his motives. But Lee Roy could handle explosives and Provo needed him especially.

Portugee Shiraz said, 'I'd surely admire to get my belly around some food.'

CHAPTER TWO

SAM BURGADE waited on the wooden kerb for a steam automobile to pitch by. He waited a while longer, until the dust from its passage had settled back down on to the unpaved surface of Meyer Avenue, and then he stepped down into the powder and walked across the intersection to J. S. Mansfield's news depot. By the time he got there, his boots had a fine film of silver dust on them, but underneath you could still make out the gloss of expensive leather.

The clerk greeted him by name, with respect, and asked after Susan, and remarked it was going to be a scorcher, and Sam Burgade nodded and said Susan was fine and yes indeed it wasn't much for wet but it was all hell for hot. After this ritual, the clerk got out Burgade's reserved copy of the morning *Star* and gravely accepted Burgade's five-cent piece in his palm, and Burgade went up the length of the block and across the street into the dim cool lobby of Orndorff's Cosmopolitan Hotel.

His crinkly outdoor eyes squinted against the dimness. He picked at the white shirt-front under his suit coat, pulling it away from his damp chest, and tipped his black hat back to cool his brow, and walked to his regular stuffed armchair by the front window. Maggie the waitress was just straightening up, having set down his saucer and cup of hot black coffee, and when she turned, sweeping a stray strand of colourless hair back from her face, she smiled and said, 'Right on time, Mr. Burgade.'

'Morning, Maggie.'

She went away towards the kitchen, smiling fondly, perhaps because she liked him, perhaps because he tipped her dependably at the end of each month when he paid his \$1.50 bill for coffee and whatever bills he had run up in the saloon bar.

By the Seth Thomas clock over the registry it was seven thirty. Sam Burgade, bored, settled his elbows on the arms of the chair, crossed his legs, laid the newspaper across his up-ended knee, and reached for his coffee without looking at it. As he ran his eyes over the various front-page adverts and headlines, he kept glancing up to see if anybody he knew had come into the lobby.

The headlines were disappointing and dull.

CARRANZA REVOLT GATHERS FORCE
IN MEXICO.

BALKAN WAR DISPATCHES:
BULGARIA ATTACKS SERBO-GREEK
POSITIONS.
RUMANIA AND TURKEY ENTER WAR
AGAINST BULGARIA.

GOV. GEORGE P. HUNT ANNOUNCES
ARIZ.
1912 COPPER OUTPUT REACHED
200,000 TONS.

PRESIDENT WILSON PROPOSES
FEDERAL RESERVE BANK SYSTEM.

SOLONS LODGE OBJECTIONS TO NEW
FEDERAL INCOME TAX.

NEW ELECTORAL REFORM LAW IN
EGYPT.

Sam Burgade swallowed a yawn, and some coffee, and blinked, and then his eyes fell on the two-column item near the bottom corner of the page:

PRISON BREAK AT YUMA: TWO
GUARDS MURDERED,
CONVICTS ESCAPE. FOURTEEN
DESPERATE MEN STILL
AT LARGE. LATEST DISPATCHES
BY TELEPHONE.

His instincts and interests stirred, he folded the paper to read the article. He took the reading glasses out of their pocket case and wiped them with methodical deliberation, hooked them over one ear at a time, and settled down to read.

Sam Burgade was a striking man, a straight-backed long-legged figure with thick white hair, deeply tanned saddle-leather face, hand-tailored black business suit, old-style wing collar and cravat, glossy black walking boots. He wore his white hair bushy at the back, in a mane. Deep creases, knotted muscularly, ran like painful wounds from the nostrils to the lip-corners of his seamed brown face. All his bones were long; he was lean, but his chest hadn't caved in with age. Eyes were the colour of quicksilver, slotted between sun-shuttered lids. He was an old man now, sixty-one, but folks still said there was moss growing down his north side. Not that it mattered much what folks said. Sam Burgade was an anachronism, all used up. There wasn't much call for over-age ex-fighting men. With the help of rich acquaintances for whom he had done work in the old days — railroad bosses, bankers, corporate managers of big stock ranches — he had run his savings and pension up into a tidy sum for his old age, but clipping coupons and living in comfort didn't make up for the boredom.

When he got up to shave each morning he was a little startled he still expected to see a young face staring back at him out of the mirror. He didn't feel old. It didn't seem so long ago he had ridden scout for Crook in the campaigns against Geronimo. Hired on with the railroad to head up their train-robber-busting crew. Gone to work for the Inca Land and Cattle Company to demolish the hole-in-the-wall outlaw towns of Jack-Mormon rustlers that made an industry out of stealing beef by the herd from the Hatchet and the Arrowhead. Headed up the Arizona Territorial Police from 1902 to 1910. Organised the militia march into Bisbee to knock the steam out of the strikers' bombings and assassinations at the great open-pit copper mines. Stumped for George Hunt in the campaign for Arizona's first governorship after statehood.

That was just last year, that campaign. But when he'd got up to make speeches the crowd had treated him like an elder statesman — courteous respect, but inattention. Look at that poor old man, son, he used to be the toughest son of a bitch in Arizona, but that was before your time, that was in the Old Days.

Life had settled into dreary ritual. Mornings in the hotel, afternoons sitting on the sheriff's front porch or playing horseshoes with the old boys who'd soon move into the Pioneers' Home, evenings in the genteel rubbed-oak-and-leather dimness of the Stockmen's Club, reminiscing about Old Times with other old-timers.

Sam Burgade was in a mood all the time now, he didn't care anymore one way or the other: a why-not mood of indifference. Nothing mattered very much. The century had turned thirteen years ago and Sam Burgade did not belong in this new one . . .

The newspaper story took him back. It was Zach Provo's name that did it. *My God, I thought he was dead.* Then he thought about it and did some arithmetic in his head, and realised Provo wasn't all that old, after all. Provo had been almost a kid when Sam Burgade ran him to earth in 1885. Provo didn't have to be much over fifty years old, even now. Think of that. Still a young man, after having spent three fifths of his life in the Yuma Penitentiary. What did a man feel like, busting out into this newfangled world after all that time?

It didn't matter much, he supposed. They'd have Provo

back soon enough. Not like the old days. In these modern times nobody could outrun the telephone and the horseless carriage, the railroads, the telegraph all over the place. The state militia up in Phoenix was even trying out one of those new flying machines.

No point fretting about Provo, anyway. Provo had got less than he deserved. He should have been hanged in the first place. He would have been, if he'd been tried by a cow-country jury instead of a crowd of city men in Phoenix who'd become soft where they sat and soft where they did their thinking. And that high-priced defence attorney pleading with the jury to take into account that Provo had already suffered grievously, been shot to pieces and had his young wife killed before his eyes: Provo had already been punished, the lawyer kept saying. He's already paid a good part of the price for whatever crimes you may decide he committed, although nobody's admitting he blew up that express car with the four men inside it; after all, this big-time railroad detective, this famous Samuel Burgade, searched every foot of the ground and every hiding place along the Navajo track line, and every inch of Defendant Provo's homestead, and never found nary a trace of that forty-eight thousand dollars in gold that my client's supposed to have stolen from that train . . .

'Hot enough for you, Sam?'

Gus Leggett's abrasive voice brough him out of his reverie. He looked up in resignation Gus Leggett was the town bore. But Gus was also the accountant who had invested Burgade's money for him, mostly on the advice of Burgade's former employers, and Gus was good-hearted.

'Hot enough,' Burgade said judiciously, and Gus seemed to take it as sufficient invitation. Gus pulled up a chair and sat down.

'I see you've been reading the paper.' Gus had a narrow body, thinning blond hair, the rheumy eyes of a bloodhound, and an infuriating tendency to chuckle at everything he said — a nervous habit; every sentence ended with an awkward, neighing laugh.

Gus beamed. 'Funny thing about old Zach Provo, isn't it? You're the one who captured him way back in the Dark Ages, aren't you, heh? I hear they captured that bunch in the farmhouse downriver from Quartzsite, but there's still nine at large, and Provo's one of them, heh. What do you think of that, now?'

'They'll get run down. They always do.'

'Maybe they got across into Mexico by now, what do you think, heh?'

'Maybe they did.'

'Not like the old days when you and the Rurales had to make a private deal because there wasn't any extradition treaty between the States and Mexico. You ever wish it was the old days again, Sam?'

'No,' he lied.

His unenthusiastic monosyllables finally penetrated Gus's awareness, and Gus stood up. 'Well,' Gus said, and trailed off, and started again, 'Well, I got to get up to the office, lot of work to do these days. Things are booming all over. You ought to stop up sometime and we can go over your portfolio, heh.'

'I'll do that.'

Gus went, hobbling a little; a colt had stomped his foot once, he had lost a toe, and after that he had taken up desk work. He hated horses — 'One end bites and the other kicks' — and hadn't ridden one in thirty years. But then, Burgade thought, *How long since I got aboard a horse?* Last year, the statehood parade. He couldn't remember a time since then.

He looked at the paper again and then, with sudden resolve, stood up and marched out on to the boardwalk, full of dignity, with the folded newspaper under his arm. He tugged his hat down and walked around the corner, where a blast of dry hot wind struck him across the quarter; tucked his face towards his shoulder and let the wind blow him down the street past the old, disused whipping post to the courthouse.

God had made Sheriff Noel Nye as ugly as He could and

then hit him in the face with a shovel. Nye had arrived in Tuscon twenty years ago like a whipped dog, a down-at-the-heels Nebraskan with one bad lung. Burgade had taken him on to do desk work and run chores. Nye had followed him on to the Territorial Police, learned the work diligently, grown robust in health, made headlines by shooting it out with one of the Clanton offshoot gangs, and got elected sheriff of Pima County on a wave of hero-worship. He had kept the job through subsequent elections by maintaining a superb record of peacekeeping, arrests, and convictions. Nye was loud and blasphemous; shaggy and folksy and garrulous on the surface, but in fact he was whip-smart. The long hair fell all over his malformed face in an effort to conceal the cauliflowered ears and forceps-elongated head; it exposed the squashed pug nose and the long pointed chin. The eyes were good eyes, warm, intelligent, the colour of rusty iron.

Nye got up and came around the desk to welcome him. 'Hot damn. Good to see you, Captain. Come on in and set.' Nye had called Burgade 'Captain' since the Territorial Police days.

'I don't mean to take up your time, Noel.' Burgade stood stiffly, embarrassed by the knowledge that he had no official capacity here any longer. The sad realisation tended to emphasise his austere demeanour; he was distant and aloof anyway, it had always been difficult for him to establish close human contacts – his closest friends were all dead and he had not made new ones. Only Burgade's daughter, Susan, remained inside the defensive shell.

Nye said impatiently, 'I always got time for you, Goddamnit — hell, Captain, I owe you everthang I — '

'That's neither here nor there. You've got work to do and if I'm in the way, just — '

'Balls. Shut up and set yoseff down, y'hear? Christ, the way you take on, Captain, you'd think you was the fucking town drunk or something. You don't never need apologise to me.'

Burgade turned the chair and sat down, at attention.

'I guess you been readin' about Zach Provo bustin' out of Yuma.'

'Yes. That's why I came. Any more word?'

'Not a whisper. That half-breed's like some kind of mirage. Him and eight others, includin' that Mixican Cesar Menendez, you recall it was him burnt down the Santa Cruz jail. Them two make a mean cocksuckin' pair.'

Burgade had the newspaper open on his lap. He adjusted his reading glasses and ran his finger down the page. 'Gant, Quesada, Weed, Shiraz, Riva, Tucker, Shelby. I remember two or three of them.'

'Some of 'em most lakly come along after your time,' Nye said, and immediately clamped his mouth shut as if he had said the wrong thing.

'Likely,' Burgade drawled evenly. 'Look, Noel, Yuma's a long way from your jurisdiction, but I had a few thoughts on this. I guess I knew Sach Provo as well as anybody at one time.'

Nye sat back. He wore a bowler hat. It was his office hat. When he went outside he always changed hats, put on an olive-drab flat-brimmed Army hat with four dents in the crown. He pushed the bowler on to the back of his head and said, 'I'll be obliged to hear it, Captain.'

'I remember Quesada and Lee Roy Tucker. Tough enough, but not long on brains. It they had split up by themselves they'd have been caught by now. Gant and George Weed, maybe they're smart enough to stay out of sight. I can't speak for the others listed here. But Quesada and Tucker, they'd have fallen into the net by now if they were on their own.'

'I think I follow your meanin', Captain, but go on.'

'Two guards dead means two guns missing. Did either gun turn up among the convicts they've recaptured?'

'No. We got a telegraph ware on that. Armed and dangerous. Ain't neither gun showed up. They was riot guns, by the way, big motherfuckin' twelve-gauges, pump-slides.

'Then it's damn good odds Zach Provo has got at least one of those guns.'

'Uh-huh. And lakly Menendez got the othern.'

'Possibly. My point is, the rest of those convicts aren't armed. They wouldn't have a prayer by themselves. They're probably sticking close to Provo.'

'Sure. Lak you say, if they wasn't all stuck together in one bunch, we'd have run a few of 'em down by now.'

'Nine men in a bunch, sticking together. That suggest anything to you, Noel?'

'Sure. I'm catching up on you, Captain. Nine men, you got to feed them, you got to get transpo't for them, you got to get them clothes.'

'And guns,' Burgade said. 'They'll have to hit someplace where they can get enough guns to equip everybody.'

'In other words, they ain't hiding out in the sticks someplace. They got to head for a town.'

'Pretty soon they do. Or a big ranch, but that's less likely — too many tough men around a working ranch, and too much chance of running into armed resistance. No. They've got to raid a town. They've only got two guns now, and not much ammunition, so they can't hold a whole town up at gunpoint. They'll go in at night, on the sly. Try to break into a gun store and a drygoods and a food store. Get themselves outfitted and then steal horses out of a livery stable.'

'You're dead right, Captain. Ain't but one way for them to do it. Of course, it could be any town between here and California, on this side of the Border or down below in Mixico.'

'No. We can narrow that down a lot more than that. They had to use the railroad, Noel. Either that or they're still in Yuma.'

Nye sat bolt upright. 'Railroad? But they done searched ever' car on ever' train in and out of Yuma.'

'Then they're still in Yuma, holed up. Or they hid somewhere on a train where nobody found them. Either way, it narrows down. West of Yuma in California what have they got? Calexico, San Diego. East of Yuma they've got Gila Bend, Phoenix Junction, on up towards Flagstaff or down this way — Tucson, Benson, Lordsburg, El Paso. But I doubt they'd go as far as El Paso on a train. Too risky, and they'd be too nervous to stay put on a train that long.'

'Then what you figure? Calexico? Right on the Border, might be the most lakly bet. Easy to crawl acrosst into Mixico.'

'I doubt it. They couldn't go anywhere from there. It's isolated. Sand-dune desert on one side and Baja California to the south — nothing down there but rocks and cactus, they'd die of thirst in that country. No. Either they went all the way to San Diego, which is doubtful, or they came east into Arizona.'

Nye scowled at him. Nye liked to bake his opinions in a slow oven before serving them up. Now he said, 'Maybe you going a little too faist. How do we know they on a train?'

'Because they've been using dogs to track them. They'd have turned up by now if they were still on foot.'

'Two rivers down there, Captain — the Gila and the Colorado. Dogs can't follow them in a river.'

'The Gila's dried up. The Colorado — they couldn't move upstream against that current, and if they moved downstream much past Yuma they'd get swept up in the tidal bore and drowned.'

'You got it all pieced out, ain't you? Jesus, I forgot how faist your mind works, Captain.'

'Then think about this. Most likely they got aboard a train. Most likely it was eastbound. Most likely they're all in a tidy bunch that ought to be fairly easy to pin down, only two shotguns among them. The first train into Tuscon from Yuma is about due into the yards — you've got about fifteen minutes to meet it, Noel, if you want to try it.'

Nye's grin split his ugly face wide. He stood up in a single motion, tossing his bowler on the desk and reaching for his campaign hat. 'Grab yoseff up that rifle there, Captain, and come on.'

Nye summoned three deputies from the wardroom on the way out of the courthouse. They commandeered the chain-driven water truck and went gnashing and bumping down to the railroad yards at a reckless speed of twenty-five miles an hour, scattering pedestrians and terrorizing horses in the streets. Burgade stood on one of the steel foot tabs alongside the sprinkler tank, like a fireman, one hand tight on the hand grip and the other, in which he carried the rifle, holding his hat on against the wind. For the first time in a year he felt eager about something.

His energy quickly dissipated in the heat and disappointment. They prowled the train with deliberate care, infuriating the engineer, who howled about the delay and insisted he had a timetable to keep. Nye said, 'You just hold on to your fucking horses and leave when I tell you you can leave.' They started with the caboose and went through every car. The engineer went petulantly along to the dispatcher's and complained about the delay, whereupon five railroad yard guards were sent along to help speed up the search, but still it was almost half an hour before Nye and Burgade got near the front of the half-mile-long freight and found the icebox car with its door a foot open.

Nye sent two deputies in first, guns up, and one of them came back to the door after a moment holding his nose expressively. 'Sun sure got to this here meat, Sheriff, but ain't no sign of nobody in here.'

Burgade said, 'Let me have a look. Give me a boost up, Noel.'

Nye cupped his interlaced hands into a stirrup and gave him a leg up. Burgade felt stiff in his joints. He stopped just inside the car to accustom his eyes to the dimness, and made his way across the stinking rows of carcasses from corner to corner.

When he came back to the open door and blew out his lungs to clear his nostrils, he had in his hand a handkerchief he had removed from his hip pocket. The corner was stained.

Nye threw his head back. 'What you got up there?'

Burgade tossed the handkerchief down to him, said 'Try a smell,' sat down on the doorframe and eased himself to the ground. His bones felt brittle.

Nye said, 'Smells like awl.'

'Light oil. Maybe gun oil.'

'Gun awl — sure, got to be.'

One of the deputies said, 'How in hell'd he find that with all that beef blood all over the place?'

'Used my eyes,' Burgade said shortly. But secretly he was pleased with himself.

'Gun awl,' Nye said. 'Like maybe from a riot gun.'

'They were here,' Burgade said. 'I'd bet my shirt on it. They got inside at Yuma and hid behind the carcasses. After the train pulled out they shoved the ice blocks outside. You might find out if the Yuma patrols found any big puddles or new-dried mud along the right-of-way this side of Yuma. They were big blocks of ice — it'd take time to evaporate; if anybody comes across it before tomorrow morning it'll probably still be damp.'

'Aeah,' Nye said slowly, working it all around in his brain. The disfigured face stirred. 'Someplace between here and Yuma, they got off this train. How many towns along the line where they'd stop or slow down enough for men to jump off? Welton, Asher, Mohawk, Aztec, Sentinel, Theba, Gila Bend, Mobile, Casa Grande, Arizola, Toltec, Eloy, Picacho, Red Rock, Marana, Rillito, Cortaro, Jaynes, Tucson. I leave anything out?'

'Maricopa,' the deputy said. 'And ain't there a little post office this side of Asher a few miles — Tack Toe, somethin' like that?'

'Tacna,' said Burgade. 'Whistle-stop.'

Nye picked at a lower front tooth with a fingernail. 'Lot of towns to cover. Some of them too small to have any local police.' He poked his finger into the deputy's chest. 'You run up to the depot and get on that telephone, Buck. Alert ever' town down the line from here to Yuma. Get a holt of Captain Rynning in Phoenix and the sheriffs in Pinal and Maricopa and Yuma counties. Tell 'em the convicts was on this train.'

Burgade walked back across town with the sheriff. Over past the Presidio Hotel and down Congress Street, with the morning sun hot on the backs of their shoulders A light traffic of vehicles and horses fogged the air with dust. Burgade carried the rifle in one fist and drew curious glances from passersby. He muttered, 'Think ahead. Think like them.'

'What's that Captain?'

He lifted his voice. 'What's their next move, Noel?'

'Hell, they git outfitted, they could head just about any which way.'

'Maybe. But Provo won't just head them out into the desert. He's too smart for that. Too easy to track out there. Somewhere they dropped off that freight. If it was before sunup — one of those towns down the Gila — they're gone from there by now. If it was nearer this end of the line they'll hole up till dark. Either way, they'll get guns, food, clothes, horses. They'll rob a few tills in whatever town they picked and they'll get a little pocket money that way, but I doubt there's enough loose cash in any of those towns to satisfy Zach Provo. He never did feel comfortable without a fortune tucked into his britches.'

'Supposedly he's still got that gold he stole off the Santa Fe Railroad. You never did fand it.'

'That gold's got to be way up past the Mogollon Rim somewhere. Navajo country. That's a hell of a long way from the S.P. line.'

Nye replied with enough of a grunt to let Burgade know he was listening, without interrupting Burgade's train of thought. They stepped down into the powder of Stone Avenue, went across and angled up Maiden Lane alleyway. Burgade was still musing out loud:

'Put yourself in Provo's shoes.'

'Listen, I'm glad I *ain't* in his shoes.'

'Think the way he thinks. He's got eight toughs tagging along with him. He can't afford to split up now, because there's too much risk one of them would get caught and lead us back to him. He's got to keep them together. That means he's got to have something to offer them.'

'Lak what?'

'Money.'

'Maybe I don't follow you, Captain.'

They came along by the Metropolitan Saloon. 'Buy you a beer, Noel?'

'Don't mand if I do.'

The room was dim, full of dark wood furnishings and the lingering smell of tobacco and whiskey. A few men sat around in boots and cowboy hats. A big Indian-Cavalry battle scene painting behind the bar. Burgade bought beers and propped his rifle muzzle-up against the front face of the bar. Hooked his boot heel on the rail and leaned on one elbow with the unconscious practice of long habit and said, 'Provo's got to promise them something. Otherwise he can't keep them together — he can't keep his eye on that many of them twenty-four hours a day. If a man wants to get clear of the law and drop out of sight, it's a lot easier to do with money. Buy good clothes that fit you right, pay for a Pullman compartment, stay over in expensive hotels — the law's not going to be looking for them in places like that. Buy a first-class passage on a steamer for Shanghai or Sydney or Capetown, or take a train down to Galveston and ship out for Lisbon or Marseille. That's the way to get free, but it takes money.'

'Go on, Captain.'

'Nine men. They've got to get their hands on a sizable pile of cash if it's going to split nine ways and still look impressive. They won't find that kind of money in the till of a general store in some whistle-stop. Provo's got to come up with fifteen or twenty thousand dollars to make those convicts sit up and listen. Otherwise he loses them.'

'I'm startin' to get your drift now.'

'Bait,' Burgade said. 'Why not give them something to shoot for?'

'Spell it out, what you got in mand.'

'Suppose we set up a fake story about a big shipment of cash arriving in the Tucson bank from the Denver mint. Get the story on the front page of all the newspapers this afternoon and make sure the newspapers are delivered to every crossroad store and whistle-stop in southern Arizona.'

Nye chugged his beer down. The mug had left a wet ring on the bar. He set it down carefully on the ring. 'I don't know, Captain. Take the lid off that kand of honey jar and a lot of flies bound to come swarming around besides Zach Provo. We could end up with the whole town full of bank robbers.'

'When you use a net you're bound to pull in a lot of innocent fish. If they're too small you just throw them back in the water, Noel. And if they're big enough and guilty enough then you've got a bonus.'

'Provo ain't stupid. He sees some story about a big shipment of cash money, he'll have to expect it's gonna be protected. He might even figure it for a trap.'

'Naturally. So let's give him a little extra bait. Put in the story that the money's coming in — oh, say, Friday morning maybe, on an armed westbound train. That ought to give Provo time to see the story, a few days to get over here to Tucson and get his crowd set up for it. And put in the story that the money's going to be trucked from the depot to the bank under guard. With me heading up the guard detail.'

'You?'

Burgade finished his beer and ascetically cleaned the foam from his lips with a bar napkin. 'Me. I'm the man killed Zach Provo's wife. I doubt that's slipped his mind. Quite the reverse. I imagine he's had nothing to brood about except that, and nothing much to do except brood about it. Offer Zach Provo a chance to kill me and he'll jump at it.'

'Oh sure. And you'll get dead. I don't like the price of that, Captain.'

'I'll have a little advantage, Noel. I'll know he's coming. I'll be looking for him.'

'But you're — ' Nye didn't finish the sentence and it was pretty clear what he had meant to say: *But you're an old man.*

'I've handled Zach Provo before,' Burgade said stiffly. 'I can do it again.'

'But it ain't your job, Captain.'

'I'm offering to make it my job.' *For God's sake can't you see how much I want this chance?*

Nye stirred. He rubbed a hand abrasively over his ugly face. 'I don't know, Captain. I'll have to thank on it.'

'Don't take too long. The papers are going to press.'

'I don't lak it.'

'Provo's too smart to get caught unless we bait him into it. You know that.'

'Aeah. Reckon I do. But I ain't sure he's worth catchin' if it's at the expense of your life.'

'Let me worry about that,' Sam Burgade said.

Nothing to do now but wait. Sweat it out and see if Provo swallowed the hook. Burgade walked home shortly before noon, taking his time in the heat. Big trees arched the street, throwing patterns of shade, and the stately old Spanish houses clung to a decaying dignity. The lawn in front of Burgade's house looked parched. He went up the tile-bordered walk and let himself in; the screen door flapped shut behind him with a weatherbeaten slap. The thick adobe walls made it cooler inside.

The gun cabinet was in the front parlour, tall like a china cabinet; the windowed maple doors were not locked, but the guns inside were chained and padlocked, to discourage errant children. Burgade opened the doors and inspected the assortment. Some of the long guns went back a long way. The .45-70, he'd had that one with him when he'd cornered Zach Provo in his hogan.

No time to reminisce about that now. The Springfield .06 was likely the best all-around rifle in the rack, but it was a bolt-action, not fast enough for close-in work in town streets. He passed it by. Same for the Mannlicher. The Winchester ·38-56 was too heavy, too long and ponderous. The ·32-20 was a toy, a squirrel gun, no good for man-size targets.

It came down to the Marlin .30-30. Lever-action carbine, short barrel, light stock, not much for long-range work but easy to manoeuvre and quick to reload.

He unlocked the chain and took it down. Found four

boxes of cartridges in the drawer, and after a moment's thought unlocked the cabinet door beneath and dragged out the old holster-belt and the black metal lockbox. He put the lockbox on the dining table and put its key into it, flipped the lid back and poked through the oiled handguns inside. The Army .45 automatic was the newest of them, a carved gilt-inlaid beauty. Presented to him with much fanfare at the banquet when he'd retired from the Territorial Police. Like a gold watch, he thought. He'd never got the hang of shooting the thing: it didn't point naturally, it kicked like a mule. Hard to hit the broad side of a barn from inside the barn. He put it back in the box and shuffled the others around. His favourite was the old .44 single-action, he'd carried that one on his hip nearly thirty years and the bluing was worn off to show for it. But old springs got brittle, like bones, and old firing pins tended to crystallise and shatter. Any piece of machinery that was too old and too much used was suspect: undependable.

Sad thought: he put them away with the old .44. He picked out the swing-cylinder ·45 double-action and slid it into the old holster and threw the tails of his jacket back to buckle the gunbelt around his hips and snug it down. At least the belt still fit. He hadn't put on an ounce in fifteen years. The belt loops contained ·44-40 cartidges and he had to replace them, methodically, one by one, with .45 centrefires. The old ·44's from the belt had turned green from leather corrosion.

The boxes of ·30-30's weighted down his jacket pocket. He walked out of the house with the Marlin rifle in the bend of his elbow and the revolver heavy along his thigh. Walked at a deliberate pace up to Stone Avenue and waited for the streetcar, and rode it all the way to the end of the line at Limberlost Road. It was hell hot. He walked on north towards the trees along the bank of the Rillito, half a mile along a twin-rutted wagon track through the scrub. Along the way he picked up an arm-load of discarded beer bottles.

He spent half an hour cruising the trees on both banks of

the riverbed. Not that he expected to find lovers sparking in broad daylight in this heat. But he didn't want stray ricochets cutting up somebody's wandering milch cow. He found no animal life bigger than gophers, and went down into the dry bed of the river. It was deep sand, pale tan in colour, marked here and there by clay bars and patches of sun-whitened pebbles. It was a wide river, two hundred feet from bank to bank, but no water where you could see it. This time of the year the water was all underneath, flowing along its underground channel beneath the riverbed. Dig down six, eight feet and you'd hit water. Come the rains in the autumn, a few hours' rain every day for two or three weeks, and the river would be full—flash floods coming down off the hills, a savage and furious torrent. But right now it was bone dry between the eight-foot-high cutbanks.

Burgade set up the empty bottles at the base of the north bank and waded across through the sand to the south side. He thumbed a cartridge into the breech of the Marlin and then filled the magazine with ammunition. Broke open the sidegate revolver and chambered six into it, and holstered it with the firing pin between the rims of two shells. He was too old a hand to get careless at this stage of his life: leave the pin over a live primer and you never knew when the thing might fall out of the holster, drop on a rock and go off.

He took his time practising, conserving his ammunition. Dry-fired more than he shot. He had to familiarise himself with the old moves and balances all over again: it had been a long time, muscles remembered but not to the exact point.

He had to quit twice to forage for beer bottles. Late in the afternoon the noise attracted an audience of half a dozen kids, who stood on the bank behind him and watched solemnly. He said hello to them, courteous and distant, and one or two of them knew who he was, passed the word around; nobody pestered him. The kids volunteered to go looking for more bottles for him and he sat in the lengthening shade while they scooted through the trees, found cans and bottles, and raced each other across the river to set up targets for him.

He was not above showing off. He finished the afternoon in a blaze of glory, like fireworks: started with his back to the targets; jacked a chamber into the Marlin; wheeled and began firing at an ear-splitting speed, so that the racket of each shot nearly blended into the next; the air was full of flying pieces of glass. When he had emptied the carbine he let it hang in his left hand while he slapped the revolver up from his hip and blazed away, holding the revolver out in front of him at eye level where you were supposed to. He didn't miss one of his six shots. When he walked away towards town the kids were watching him as if he were William S. Hart. He didn't let them see his pleased little smile.

His ears were still whistling and ringing when he walked up to his front door and went inside. Susan appeared at the kitchen door and began to say something, and saw his guns and stared.

'Just practising,' he said. 'Up on the Rillito. I had to wait awhile for the tram car. Didn't realise it was getting so late.'

'I've waited supper for you.' She pushed her lower lip forward to blow hair off her forehead. 'Lay off your things and get washed up.'

'Yes, ma'am,' he said drily. Susan grinned impudently. He put the guns in the front parlour, leaving them out because after supper he would clean them and oil them; he went upstairs, feeling very light on his feet, and worked the pump handle to bring water up to the second-storey tank before he went into the bathroom they had built four years ago.

His clothes were covered with dust. He chastised himself for not having changed into old clothes before he went out to shoot. He had to change; it wouldn't do to sit down to supper in dusty garb.

When he came down she said crossly, 'It's getting cold. Maybe I'd better warm it up in the oven.'

'No. I don't mind.' He held her chair for her and then went to his place at the head of the table. As he sat down he saw she was looking at the grandfather clock. He said, 'If you're going out tonight I'm sorry I held you up.'

'There's time,' she said. 'Maybe I'll cancel it anyway.'
'The Brickman fellow?'
'Yes.'
'He's a good man, you don't want to keep putting him off.'
She said, 'Quit trying to marry me off.'
'Time you got another man, Susan. Time you got married again.'

She was thirty-one, a tall girl with big eyes and good bones, high strong cheeks, a full expressive mouth. He was too close to her to know whether she was pretty but he'd heard men make admiring remarks about her. She had long hair that shone in the lamplight, dark brown hair like his own had been before it went white; her eyes were dark and dramatic and she had a soft contralto voice, low and smoky. Winters she taught fifth grade; summers she kept the books of the city police department. Nine years ago, to Burgade's intense displeasure, she had married an unambitious young deputy sheriff named Ned Hayes; Burgade had only slowly, and grudgingly, realised Hayes's virtue — he was steady, honest, dependable, not as dull as he looked at first glance, and had a good chance of making under-sheriff and possibly even sheriff. Burgade had finally learned to like him and had taken Hayes under his wing, teaching him the bits and pieces of wisdom he had picked up along the backtrail of his experience. Two years ago last month Hayes had made under-sheriff. A fortnight later Hayes had been shot dead by a store burglar when he'd stopped to investigate on his way home from a night of card-playing at the Cosmopolitan.

Burgade had brought Susan back home with him. She had cried her grief out but she'd composed herself rather quickly after the funeral — perhaps too quickly. He had a feeling some of it was still bottled up inside her. Very matter-of-fact, she'd gone to work, organised the household, mothered him insufferably, and made utterly no efforts to resume the social contacts she'd had before her husband's death. Her old friends, her age, had come around to see her but she had greeted them with exact courtesy, nothing more, and they came around less and less frequently. She encouraged no beaux. Once in a while a young man made a determined attempt to get through to her. The most recent was a young mining engineer, Hal Brickman, who had a clean-cut college-dude appearance and usually went around in baggy riding breeches and a snap-brim Eastern hat. Brickman had a good heart and a quick mind; maybe he wasn't the kind of tough outdoorsman who'd always run in the Burgade family (Sam Burgade's forebears had fought in four American wars, explored the Northwest with Lewis and Clark, trapped with Carson and Sublette, trailed cattle with Chisum) but he was solid, substantial, steady, sturdy — and Susan was thirty-one years old, and all these things weighed in Sam Burgade's considerations.

In reply to his remark about getting married she said, 'I wish you'd quit trying to run my life, Father.'

'I'm not telling you what to do. I'm telling you what in my judgment you ought to do. There's a difference.'

'I don't love Hal Brickman.'

'Seems he loves you,' he said. 'Maybe at your age you ought to stop looking to find a storybook romance and settle for something that could turn out to be just as good in the long run — a steady man who loves you and a kid or two to raise and love.'

'It terrifies you to think of me drying up into an old-maid spinster, doesn't it?'

'Susie, I'm an old man and I know about loneliness. I don't wish it for you.'

Her expression changed; she looked away quickly, addressed herself busily to her meal. Her lashes covered her eyes but he thought he had seen a moist glint in them. He pushed his chair back and held his arms stiff, braced against the edge of the table. Full of sudden low anger he said, 'God-damnit, Susie, I will not have you waste your young life looking after a tired old man like me. I had no intention of letting that comment about loneliness give you any excuse to think I need you to look after me for the rest of my life. I can damn well take care of myself. I did while you were married.'

'You were younger then,' she said in a small voice, not looking up.

'When I'm too old and feeble to look after myself,' he roared, 'I'll move myself into the goddamn Pioneers' Home.'

'Don't blaspheme, Father.'

He snorted. 'I will not have it.'

She looked up finally. 'You'll have to throw me out, then.'

'Don't think I won't.'

'Then go ahead. Do it.' Her eyes blazed.

Their glances locked: they scowled furiously at each other until Burgade's nose twitched, his lip-corner turned up, and suddenly they were both laughing helplessly. He laughed till his stomach hurt; he had to get his breath, and then he dropped his napkin on the table and went to the sideboard and got down the cognac. Rothschild 1887. He poured two snifters.

'Here. Belt that down and listen to me.'

'You old tyrant.'

'Yeah.' He sat down and a crafty gleam came into his eye. 'You know what I'm going to do? I'm going to put this house up for sale.'

'What? The house? But —'

'I know. You were born here. Well, that was a long time ago. The house is too big, we don't need it. It just keeps you hopping. I'm going to sell it.'

'And do what?'

He grinned at her. 'Move into a flat in Orndorff's Hotel.'

She glared at him, but she was amused. 'You old stinker.'

'Yeah. Won't be room for you there, Susie. I'll have maids to keep my room clean and a whole hotel kitchen to cook for me. I won't need the likes of you fussing around after me.'

'You're bluffing,' she said, 'but I love you.'

'I am not bluffing. Next week the house goes up for sale.'

'Do it if you want,' she said, feigning indifference. 'But

don't do it on my account. If you really can't stand having me around, I'll leave. You don't have to sell the house.'

'Is that a promise?'

'It is if you're asking for it.'

Loneliness pressed at him from unseen shadows. But he said, 'I'm asking for it.'

She was studying her hands, turning them over, again and again as if they were unfamiliar objects she'd never seen before. 'All right,' she said in the same small voice. 'All right, Father. But it doesn't mean I'm going to marry Hal.'

The door clapper banged three or four times. Burgade put down his brandy snifter. 'That'll be your young man. Better get your shawl — there'll be a cool breeze along the river tonight.'

Her eyes flashed. 'What makes you think we'd go walking in that notorious lovers' lane?'

He only grinned at her. Colour filled her cheeks and she went out of the room in a rush. But he noticed she was moving with a light step. Still smiling, he went to the hall door and greeted Hal Brickman while Susan dashed upstairs to get her wrap. Hal wore the customary jodhpurs and engineers' boots, a charro jacket and a necktie; he had his snap-brim hat in his hand; his hair was slicked back, parted down the middle. A real dandy — but amused by it, not serious about it. Burgade didn't understand dudes very well but he liked Hal. They sat in the parlour with brandy and talked weather and crime until Susan came down, her hair freshly brushed and shining, her mother's lace shawl about her shoulders. She looked a little like her mother — not much, but enough to send Burgade's memory back twenty years.

Hal was saying, 'I imagine they'll catch them before the week's out.'

Hearing the last of it as she entered, Susan said, 'Catch who?'

'Oh, just some convicts who broke out of the penitentiary,' Hal said.

'Oh,' she said, not interested. She came into the room and Burgade rose gallantly from his chair; she pecked his cheek and let Hal take her arm and guide her towards the door. Hal said, 'Good night, sir.'

'Always good to see you,' Burgade said.

Susan hesitated. The pink tip of her tongue quested her mouth corner. 'Would you like anything from Porter's store? It'll still be open.'

'No. Nothing, thank you. And if I did I could get it myself.'

'Don't be cranky,' she said tartly. 'Nothing — that's your trouble right now, you know. You want nothing.'

Not altogether true, he thought. Right now he wanted Zach Provo. Or perhaps what he wanted was the excitement of the challenge.

They stood a moment in uncomfortable silence, Susan reluctant to leave, until Burgade turned and stared rudely at the bookcase, as if dismissing them from his mind and looking for something to read.

'Well,' Susan said uncertainly, 'good night, then, Father.'

' 'Night,' he mumbled, and took a step closer to the bookcase.

His daughter went out with her young man. Through the window he watched them go along the walk under the gaslight poles. In response to something Hal said, Susan laughed with an open throat; she seemed healthy and girlish, she touched the ground with toes like musical notes. Burgade saw Hal slip his arm around her waist.

He took down the guns and began to clean them. The air in the room was still and close: stale, as if it hadn't moved for a long time. Full of loneliness. Burgade spread the pieces of the guns on a sheet of newspaper; he sat cross-legged on the floor like an Indian and wiped each bolt and spring and cam with an oily scrap of cloth. The room seemed to grow larger and quieter. In his mind he tried to reconstruct a portrait of Zach Provo. It had been twenty-eight years and the image was difficult to resurrect. Perhaps the man had lost his hair, although that wasn't common among Navajos. But then Provo wasn't full-blooded. Perhaps he had gone to fat — but that was hard to credit. The face had been bladed like a hatchet. Hard sinister eyes like two holes burned into a hide. Skin the hue of tarnished copper. It was coming back: the long jaw you could scratch a match on, the heavy black eyebrows, the lean slightly hunched body with its tense quickness of long-corded musculature. A man like that, how much would he change in twenty-eight years? Had prison collapsed the mouth, faded the eyes, thinned the hair, made the hard brown body flabby? Changed the tough, taut, commanding presence into flaccid weakness? It wasn't possible. Not Provo. A man like that, hardship wouldn't grind down; it would only polish him up, like hard steel against a grindstone.

But maybe that was just a hope. Maybe he wanted Provo to be faster and tougher than ever. To increase the challenge.

I'm going to nail him, Sam Burgade thought, but he felt a little ashamed. He didn't hate Zach Provo; he didn't really care one way or the other about Provo. It was only that Provo gave him something to think about besides lonely old age.

I hope they don't get him before I get a crack at him.

CHAPTER THREE

PROVO stood in the open door of the labourer's shack watching the lights of Gila Bend, waiting for Menendez to return. There was always the chance Menendez wouldn't come back at all, would just light out and keep going. But he didn't think so. He'd put a bug in Menendez's ear about that Santa Fe gold cache up on the Mogollon and he had a feeling Menendez would stick to him like a saddleburr until Menendez got near that money.

The two Mexican labourers who occupied the shack had showed up just after dark. Provo had let them come inside and then jumped them. Portugee had wanted to kill them with their own knives but Provo had called him off: leave a trail of corpses and they'd only bring more trouble down on their heads — Pinkertons, the Army. The labourers lay back in a corner, trussed with their own belts and ripped-up shirts, gagged, sweating their terror into the stifling suffocation of the hot overcrowded room.

It was a long wait and Provo got uneasy. But somewhere around midnight Menendez came from town, riding a horse at a skittish walk. There was a heaped bundle tied on behind the saddle. For a moment Provo wasn't sure — he kept inside the dark doorway with his riot gun ready — but it was Menendez all right.

Menendez drew rein by the door. Up close in the starlight Provo could see he was wearing range clothes, Levi's and a plaid shirt, and his ankle irons and chains were gone. Menendez's waistline bulged with four or five gunbelts and holstered handguns.

Provo said, 'Can't you hold that horse still?'

Taco Riva squeezed out through the door past him. 'Let me have him.' Taco's passion was horses. He spoke soothingly and rubbed the horse's face before he took a gentle grip on the bridle.

Menendez dismounted. 'Damn town's crawling with law.'

'We've got to expect that.' Provo helped carry the heavy poncho-wrapped booty inside. 'You did fine.'

'Bet your ass I did. I hit the es-smithy first. Got us three hacksaws and all the spare blades I could ef-find. I had to cot my chains off before I could move on — sonoma bitches was making enough racket to wake the dead, and there's a focking deputy on every damn corner in town. That there bondle's clothes, shirts and pants. Took 'em out of the storeroom behind the dry-goods. Got these gons there too — only ones I could ef-find. I din' dare go near the gonsmith es-shop, there was a deputy right out ef-front.' He chuckled. 'This town goeen to be plenty pozzled in the morning.'

There was an hour of cursing and painful hacksawing before they got rid of the leg irons. Some of the clothes didn't fit too well but they'd do for openers, Provo judged. He buckled on two of the revolvers and slung a third one across his shoulders like a bandoleer. Lee Roy took offence. 'What about the rest of us, for Christ's sake?'

'I'll pass the ordnance around when I'm good and ready, Lee Roy.'

'Shee-yit.'

Provo said to Menendez, 'You scout the livery barn?'

'No good, Zach. Too much law around there. But there's ten, twelve horses in the ranch stable half a mile north of town, across the tracks. That's where I es-stole this one.'

'Then that's where we go now. Lead the way.'

Slow and easy. He let Taco go into the stable alone and saddle up eight horses; Taco was good enough with horses not to raise a ruckus. When he came out of the dark maw of the stable he crouched down by Provo and whispered, 'Mos'ly tired old horses, Zach. Tame and slow — but what you expect on a dairy ranch?'

'They'll do. All set?'

They rode out, swinging wide around Gila Bend; rode south all night, into the Saucedas, and at dawn raised the smoke of a country store's cookfire. The place squatted in a little nest of spring-fed trees in the barren rock mountains. Provo went in at gunpoint, surprised the old storekeeper and his two hired hands, and called the men in. They tied up the locals and ate a huge meal. Provo ate by himself in the kitchen, reading the newspaper Menendez had picked up in Gila Bend last night. His face changed as he read.

They took what they wanted and made off with all the money in the place — ninety dollars — and drove off all the horses and mules, to set the locals afoot and insure it would take two or three days for word to get out that they had passed this way. Provo led them out southwards, towards Ajo, and kept to that course until they had gone well beyond sight of the country store. Then he turned east along a hard-pan flat where hoof-marks would be hard to track. Sooner or later the pursuit would get to the country store back there; Provo wanted the law left with the impression the fugitives had struck due south for the Mexican Border.

They nooned somewhere on the northern quadrant of the Papago Reservation with Tabletop Mountain in sight to the northeast. It was all rock and scrub here, worthless land beaten by the furious sun. Provo's eyes were gritty from lack of sleep: he'd been up fifty-odd hours. They slept the rest of the day, Provo trading off sentry hours with Menendez. The rest of the crowd seemed too bone-tired to complain about anything.

Towards sundown he got up and stretched, hearing the ligaments crack, and walked off a piece with Menendez. He showed him the three-column story on the front page. Menendez read it laboriously, his lips moving. Finally he said,

'Oh, sure. Sure.'

'Yeah,' Provo said. 'Eighty thousand dollars with Sam Burgade guarding it.'

'Ain't no co-een-cidence, Zach. You know it's a focking trap.'

'Sure. That's the way the old bastard's mind works.'

'They can't catch us so they want to draw us into Tucson.' Menendez pronounced it the Spanish way, *Took-sohn*. 'They'll be waiting with every gon in town.'

'Be a shame to disappoint old Sam Burgade, wouldn't it.'

Menendez blinked at him. 'You ain't seriously thinking about goeen in there, Zach.'

'Not into Burgade's trap, no. But we're going into Tucson.'

'You got your brains op your ass or what? They're waiting for us with everything they got.'

'They're waiting for us to hit that so-called money shipment. Friday morning when Burgade picks it up at the train depot and trucks it over to the bank. What'll you bet there ain't no real money at all? Just an empty box for them to lug along to make it look good.'

'Sure. So why you talking about Tucson?'

'Because come Friday morning, every gun in town will be lined up at the depot and along Congress Street and at the bank. They'll have every inch of that street covered. You know what that's got to mean. It means they've got to pull deputies and bank guards off every other cash vault in town. Off the express office, off the mercantile savings-and-loan, off the hotel cash tills and the company payroll offices. Friday's payday, right?'

Menendez smiled slowly. 'If you don't beat all, Zach.'

It was then Tuesday evening. They spent the next forty-eight hours moving into position and equipping themselves according to Provo's plan. Thursday afternoon they made camp in Rose Canyon, in the Santa Catalinas fifteen miles northeast of Tucson. A crystal creek trickled down from canyons higher up, crowding the defile with greenery; it was cool among the trees. Provo sent young Mike Shelby into Tucson to reconnoitre – Shelby was the one least likely to be recognised, he looked like any honest dumb young cowboy, and Provo could trust him to come back. Provo had spent an hour in Tucson last night, after dark, riding the back streets of the mercantile and warehouse sections, scouting targets. He had kept his coat collar up and his hat-brim down and nobody had paid him any attention. He had even drifted along the street within a block of Sam Burgade's house, scouting the place out. He'd had plenty of time in Yuma to read every newspaper scrap about Burgade over the past twenty-eight years, and he'd picked the brains of every new prisoner. He knew a lot about the man, considering he hadn't seen him in twenty-eight years. He knew where Burgade lived and what his daily habits were. He knew Burgade's daughter lived in and kept house for the old man. He even knew that on Friday mornings Susan stayed home from her part-time job to do her thorough weekly house-cleaning and laundry.

They had outfitted themselves in various village stores, going in in pairs, not attracting attention, buying what they needed with the cash they'd pilfered from the country store back in the Saucedas. Menendez wore an old straw hat that had turned an uneven brown — he'd stolen it off the hat rack in a café in Marana yesterday noon. Provo wore black stovepipe boots up to his knees, an old-fashioned brown liner duster that came down as far as the boot tops, and a peaked five-gallon hat. It was a sinister costume and he'd picked it for effect. Portugee and Lee Roy had lifted what explosives they needed from a mining construction shack up near Oracle in the Catalinas, and Menendez had augmented the arsenal with rifles and revolvers from the back room of a Marana gun shop. The theft would have been discovered by now but nobody had any reason to connect it with the fugitive convicts.

Shelby arrived at sunset, dismounted, and turned his horse over to Taco Riva. He reported:

'You were right, Zach, our best bet's got to be the smelter mill. It's away over west of town, a mile west of the area they'll guard when the train comes in, and it looks like they're gonna pull the guards off it for the train depot. They got a big old safe in the back room behind the paymaster's office and I guess they must keep a pretty good wad inside — they pay off every first and third Friday of the month and tomorrow's the third Friday in July. Four-, five-hundred man payroll — got to be at least twenty thousand dollars in there. Be easy to move in and out if we come down through the canyon back of the smelter. Right up to the back door of the paymaster's office. Won't be but half a dozen men in sight of us and none of them armed.'

Provo stood back against a tree, thumbs hooked in the front pockets of his trousers. His face was hard, ungiving, a blue-steel hatchet. 'Then there it is, you gents. Twenty thousand to split – more than two thousand apiece. A man can go a long way on two thousand dollars. What do you say?'

Lee Roy said, 'You asking us or telling us?'

'I'm asking you now, Lee Roy. I can't force you all to help me rob the paymaster.'

'Then how come you din' ask us before?'

'I had to keep us together. It was no time to take a vote.'

George Weed said, 'Hell, quit jawing. We're all with you, Zach. And if Lee Roy don't like it he'll get all eight of us on his neck.'

Lee Roy said sarcastically, 'I'm real timid, George. I'll shake like a leaf if you threaten at me again.'

'Gentle down,' Provo murmured. 'I'm going to pass the guns around later tonight and I don't want you people using them on each other.'

Lee Roy's feral face became crafty. Provo knew what he was thinking. Well, that was all right. He wasn't going to give Lee Roy any guns, but Lee Roy didn't have to know that until the last minute. In the meantime the anticipation would keep him quiet.

'It's going to take timing and brains,' Provo told them. 'First off, we've got to time it to go with the train schedule. This so-called money train pulls in tomorrow morning at nine. We'll hit the smelter paymaster not later than ten minutes after nine. Now, at nine o'clock exactly, Mike Shelby's going to be on the Casa Grande road northwest of Tuscon and Quesada's going to be on the Benson road east of town. At four or five minutes after nine you two will cut the telephone and telegraph wires at both ends of town. That's what we stole these two-dollar watches for. Now, once you've cut the wires you'll ease around wide and make your way right back here where we stand now. This is where we'll meet afterwards. Right here at noon sharp. Then we divvy up the money and go our separate ways. Meantime, while these two are cutting the wires, the rest of — '

Quesada said, 'How do you cut through them wires, Zach? Them poles hard to climb.'

'No trouble. They only run seventeen poles to the mile, Joaquim. The rest's held up by cactus and mesquite. You'll find a low spot easy enough. Use your hacksaw.'

Quesada gritted his neat white teeth. The back of his neck was red. He sat down, grunting with burly effort, losing interest in the rest.

Provo said, 'Will Gant rides down below the smelter to cut the telephone line between the smelter and town. That leaves six of us. We go into the paymaster's office and tie everybody up, with gags. Lee Roy blows the safe open with the blasting gear. We clean it out and get to our horses fast. When we light out, we head down the road and pick up Will Gant and cut straight across the north side of Tucson.'

Lee Roy said, 'You crazy in the head. Right acrosst the damn town? Why not fade back into them mountains back of the smelter?'

'Because I say so, Lee Roy.'

At four in the morning he kicked them awake and passed the guns out. When Lee Roy didn't get one there was a dangerous moment. Lee Roy exploded in a few choice phrases and tensed his bony fists. Provo had to level a gun on him. 'You'll have your hands full with blasting powder.'

'That ain't no goddamn call to — '

'Shut up, Lee Roy. If you want me to spell it out, I don't want you behind me with a gun. I don't trust your hillbilly ass, understand? You don't need a gun. Just blow the safe, that's your job. It's worth better than two thousand dollars to you.'

'How do I know you ain't gonna kill me after?'

'If I was going to kill you, Lee Roy, I wouldn't have dragged you along all this way alive, would I,' he lied.

Will Gant took Lee Roy by the arm and spun him around. 'Quit acting like a fool.'

Lee Roy stalked off to his horse in high dudgeon. Provo caught a corner of Menendez's dry glance in the starlight, and wheeled his horse. 'All right. Let's move.'

There was always the chance a horse would throw a shoe and go lame, or some other delay would crop up. Provo gave it plenty of time to cover possibilities. They reached the canyon behind the smelter a full hour ahead of time. He checked his watch and dismounted them, eased himself down with his back against a rock, and felt idleness trickle through his muscles. Lee Roy's resentful glance lay against him, harsh and baleful; Provo ignored it. Menendez crouched right beside Provo and spoke low:

'This idea of yours, goeen right across Tucson after we pull it off. That got something to do with Burgade?'

Maybe.'

'Ahjess. I din' figure you was goeen to let him off that easy. Bot I don' want my ass hung on Burgade's account, Zach.'

'Ain't nobody's ass going to be hung.'

'You ain't maybe thinking of goeen looking for Burgade, are you?'

'No.'

'I thought you wanted him.'

'I intend to skewer the bastard,' Provo said, 'but that doesn't mean I'm stupid enough to go gunning for him right in the middle of that posse of his.'

'Then you got me pozzled, Zach.'

Provo smiled. 'I never said I aimed to shoot him, did I. I spent twenty-eight years coming to this — I don't aim to let him off easy with a bullet. He's going to sweat his balls off before I'm done with him. He's going to bleed slow and long. I told you before — I'm going to peel him down to a whimper.'

'Ahjess. But how?'

'You ask a lot of questions, don't you.'

'I don't like surprises, Zach.'

'You just take care of Lee Roy when the time comes. Let me worry about the rest.'

'It ain't Lee Roy I'm worried about. It's you.'

Provo smiled a little. 'Just trust me, amigo. You'll get rich.'

Menendez spat out of the side of his mouth. 'I don't trost nobody, Zach You know that.

'You could always get your horse and ride out. Why not do that, right now?'

Menendez smiled. 'You want that?'

'No. I need you to help me keep an eye on the rest of these fools.'

'That's what I thought,' Menendez said, but he didn't press it further.

Provo kept checking his snap-lid watch. Presently it was time. He stood up. 'All right. Let's put it in the saddle.'

Provo split them up at the head of the road. Gant rode down first, bypassing the smelter, heading for the telephone line where it sagged across the creek half a mile below. Provo took Lee Roy with him and split the rest of them up, to drift in from various directions so as to avoid attention.

The smelter was a sprawl of smoke-greyed structures, conveyor ramps, shacks, corrugated roofs, a fifty-foot smokestack that spewed a rancid cloud into the sky. The last stragglers of the 8.00 a.m. shift were trudging into the buildings, big men in grey coveralls and railroad-style caps. Outside the manager's building on the hill above the plant stood five or six parked chain-driven trucks and two open horseless carriages. That was where the paymaster's office was. There was a pay window at the side of the building and a well-worn foot track where the men queued up for their pay. Beyond, to the north, was a neighbouring sand-and-gravel operation, making a great racket. Provo sent Lee Roy out in front of him and they rode downslope towards the back door of the manager's building. They dipped into a canyon and lost sight of the building, but the tall smoke-eruptive stack was still in view above the intervening hump of cactus-clumped ground. A few fleece-ball clouds drifted across the sun; it wasn't as hot as it had been yesterday.

They tethered the horses in a cutbank-arroyo thirty yards behind the building. As far as Provo could tell, no one had remarked their arrival. Shortly Taco Riva rode in from the far end of the arroyo and dismounted, staying put to hold the horses. Portugee and George Weed came up from the direction of the sand-and-gravel quarry, Weed looking like a black sack of potatoes in the saddle: he was no horseman. Finally Menendez showed up. 'Ain't got moch time now, Zach.'

'Too much time gives a man whiskers.' Provo snapped his watch open. One minute after the hour. He could hear a train hooting in the distance; the train was a couple of minutes late but that didn't matter, Tucson's attention would be focused on Congress Street right about now, and that was fine.

Provo cast an eye at Lee Roy. 'Got everything you need?'

'I reckon,' Lee Roy said reluctantly.

'You know how to set the charges, don't you?'

'Ain't no call for you to tell me how to handle my binness, Zach.' Lee Roy heaved the burlap gunnysack on to his shoulder as if it contained harmless tools instead of highly volatile blasting gear.

Portuguee Shiraz unholstered both his .45 Army automatic pistols. The damn things bothered Provo for no good reason other than his ignorance of them; he had no familiarity with newfangled handguns, but Portugee claimed he could handle them fine. The Negroid lips peeled back on his black vulpine face in an expression that was more spasm than smile.

The roots of Provo's hair were damp with sweat but his hands were rock steady. He swept them all with his ungiving face. 'Let's go, then.'

Provo went across first, with Portugee. They moved quickly, bent double: up the cutbank, across the flats through the brush, up shoulderblade-flat against the wall beside the back door.

No one inside the building gave any alarm. There was only one window on this side anyhow — possibly a latrine or storeroom. Provo made an arm signal and two heads appeared at the lip of the cutbank. Weed and Lee Roy came humping it over the edge, Menendez right behind them. They came in tight, sweating, and Provo nodded to Portugee. Portugee palmed the latch of the door and tested it. It wasn't locked. He swung it open and went in. Provo twisted through the doorway right behind him and braced the riot gun against his hip.

They were in a clerical office — four desks: two woman secretaries, a clerk type in a green eyeshade, and a middle-aged man at the back desk in shirtsleeves and mining-engineer boots.

'Not a word out of anybody,' Provo hissed, 'or you get dead.'

Shock and terror chased each other across the four startled faces. Menendez whipped inside and strode across the office to the nearest door; wrenched it open and went in gun first.

One of the women started to babble something incoherent in a tiny falsetto voice. Portugee took two long strides and clapped his palm over her mouth, digging his thumb and fingers into her cheeks, holding his big .45 auto on the others. Weed sidled towards the front of the room to post himself on the front door.

Menendez came out of the back office prodding a man at gunpoint. That had to be the paymaster. The man was loose-fleshed, florid, overweight, pale hair going thin over a pink scalp. He was swallowing in regular spasms and his eyes looked like the fishy popeyes of a hyperthyroid victim.

Provo wheeled to the door near him and pulled it open. It was a closet, filled with shelves of order blanks and stationery. He pushed it shut and moved deeper into the room.

Portugee Shiraz took his hand away from the woman's mouth. She scrubbed her lips violently but didn't make a sound. Portugee said, to no one in particular, 'Everybody stay quiet like a mouse and nobody gets theirselves hurt.'.

Provo said, 'We're going to tie you up and put gags in your mouth.' He talked in a very low voice; he didn't know how thin the walls were, or how many others were in the building. 'Don't fight us and we won't hurt you.'

Lee Roy put down his gunnysack and produced cut-up lengths of rope and wads of rags. Provo and Menendez kept guns on everybody while Portugee and Lee Roy went around tying them up. It didn't take long. They tied everybody in the back corner of the office and left them there on the floor — everybody but the paymaster. Portugee knotted the paymaster's hands behind his back and prodded him in the kidney with the muzzle of the automatic. The paymaster stumbled forward.

Provo said, 'Where's the safe? Back in that room?'

'Ye-yes. But you won't — '

'Please don't tell me I'll never get away with it,' Provo said. 'Just give us the combination.' He was walking the man into the back office as he spoke.

The vault was built into the back wall. Big, substantial, with wheels on it like steamship valves. There were two big combination dials.

The paymaster whimpered and Provo struck him along the cheek with the barrel of his gun. 'Quit it. The combination. I ain't going to ask again.'

'I've only g-g-got half of it, mister. I swear to God. The company manager, he's got the combination to the other d-dial.'

'And where's this company manager?'

'D-d-d-down at the depot.'

It didn't surprise Provo. He propelled the paymaster back to the outer office. 'Tie him down and gag him. Lee Roy, in here. Get to work.'

Lee Roy lugged his sack in and looked around. 'Sheeyit. That's a big 'un.'

'Don't stand there griping. Just blow it.'

'Will you quit awderin' me around Zach? Jesus.' Lee Roy studied the furniture. 'Reckon I'll have to back that big desk up against it to shape the charge. Christ, Zach, I'm gonna have to use all the blastin' powder — it'll make a cocksucker of a noise.'

'Get busy,' Provo said, and went back to the outer office. He set his hip on the corner of a desk and talked mildly at the four bound-and-gagged prisoners. 'In a few minutes my associate's going to blow up that vault in there. You'll know when it's coming. When you do, I suggest you open your mouths and breathe easy through your mouths. Otherwise the explosion might bust your eardrums. Hear?'

Portugee shoved the paymaster down on the floor with the other four. Then he went over by the front door with George Weed and stood there cleaning his finger nails with the point of an ugly-looking knife he'd taken off a Mexican in the shack in Gila Bend. Portugee was never comfortable without a knife in his hand.

One of the women was fat and middle-aged. Her swollen cheeks were wet with tears; she was whimpering like an injured animal through the gag in her mouth. Provo glanced at her with his ungiving face but said nothing.

It seemed a long time. Sweat trickled down Provo's spine inside his shirt and linen duster. Menendez walked across the room and propped the back door fully open, and then came into the centre of the room and stood slant-eyed, watching the door where Lee Roy would appear when Lee Roy's job was done.

Portugee said to George Weed, 'Sure takin' his fucking time in there.' The two black-skinned men stood watching the front door; Weed grunted but made no other answer.

One of the prisoners was breathing hard in asthmatic rasps. Provo went over to make sure the gag wasn't choking him, but it was just fear that made the clerk wheeze. The eyes blinked like semaphores. Provo said mildly, 'Take it easy, nobody's going to shoot you,' and ambled back to the desk.

Portugee said, 'They seen our faces. They can identify us.'

'It's all right,' Provo said. 'Burgade will figure out who done this quick enough anyway.' He smiled just a little. It occurred to him to go over and open the window inside the storage closet, but he didn't bother; the blast would probably knock some walls down anyway, and everybody within miles would hear it. That was all right, too. He wanted noise.

In time Lee Roy appeared in the doorway. 'All rat. I'm fixin' to light the fuse. Won't give us more'n about ten seconds. Everybody get behint some kand of cover. Leave me a space by that desk there.' He turned around and disappeared back into the office.

Provo caught Menendez's eye and nodded slightly. Then he went across the room and wedged himself under the knee hole of the desk by the trussed prisoners. 'Take it easy now,' he told them. 'Remember what I said — open your mouths.'

Lee Roy came skittering into the room and dived behind the desk beside Menendez. Portugee and Weed were down behind cover somewhere near the front of the room. Provo shut his eyes and opened his mouth and breathed shallowly, waiting nervelessly.

The explosion knocked him back, rapped his head painfully against the underside of the desk. The ear-splitting thunder beat strident echoes around the enclosed space. There was an immediate smell of plaster dust and sawdust, very hot and acrid, mixed with a sulphur stink of cordite powder. Provo sneezed. Things were still falling down, making noise. He crawled out from under the desk and heard the relatively quiet crack of a small-calibre gunshot. He didn't glance towards Menendez. 'Come on.' He scuttled towards the office door. Menendez came to his feet beyond the desk and Provo could see Lee Roy's boots lying on the floor beyond it; the boots didn't move. Weed and Portugee stood up and faced the front door to drive away whoever came to investigate the godawful noise. Provo curled into the smoke, barked his shin against a chair leg, batted smoke with his hand, and climbed across wreckage into the big vault. Lee Roy had done his job well. The door had been smashed. Menendez said, '*Chingado*, what a mess.'

It was hard to breathe in the thick-hanging dust. Provo was untangling empty gunnysacks from under his coat. He passed two of them to Menendez and climbed into the vault.

He heard a sudden volley of gunshots, a flurry of voices bellowing in surprise and anger. Provo beat his way through the smoke. Menendez said, 'Where's all the focking money?'

'In here.' He coughed. Picked up the black steel cashbox and passed it to Menendez. The rest was scorched documents and ore samples. Menendez began to curse in a lack-lustre monotone.

'Come on then,' Provo said.

'*Leche*.' Menendez scooped the little handful of greenbacks out of the lockbox and tossed the box away. 'We been dobble-crossed.'

'Burgade,' Provo said. 'Burgade put them up to it.' He stumbled out of the smoke. Sunlight lanced down in dusty beams through a ragged hole in the roof. Part of the ceiling hung sagging across the corner above the vault, ready to fall in. Provo tripped on wreckage and almost went to his knees; wheeled into the room beyond and levelled his gun.

Portugee and Weed were forted up behind a desk, training their guns on the front door. It was punctured by half a dozen holes, bullet-size. Provo said, 'Back way. Come *on*.'

Menendez sprited across to the back door, put his head out, looked both ways and said. 'Hokay. Portugee — George.' There wasn't any need to call Lee Roy's name. Lee Roy lay seeping into the floorboards where Menendez had shot him.

Portugee put a bullet through the front door and whooped and ran for the back at George Weed's heels. Provo crossed the room, firing deliberately into the front door. He spared the trussed prisoners a single glance and Lee Roy's corpse none; went out with knuckles wrapped white around his gun and broke into a flat low run, zigzagging.

The others were ahead of him, leaping over the cutbank and dropping from sight into the arroyo. Provo was halfway across when Menendez's head popped up at the rim. A gun at the outside corner of the building opened up on Provo and some fool's voice yelled at him to halt. Menendez drove the shooter back with a furious blaze of fire and Provo went over the rim in a flat dive. He somersaulted acrobatically and hit the soft clay bed on his feet; stumbled, got his footing, and scrambled towards the horses.

Taco Riva held the animals patiently; passed out pairs of reins as methodically and unperturbedly as a school-teacher passing out test papers. 'Where's Lee Roy?'

'Not coming,' Provo said, winded. 'But bring his horse along.' He swung up into the saddle, keeping bent over low. Menendez fired a final shot and sprinted for his saddle. Weed and Taco were getting mounted. Provo sank his heels hard into horse flanks: the horse broke into an immediate flaying gallop, throwing back clots of earth. He neck-reined savagely around in the centre of the arroyo and ran uphill, firing back over his shoulder at the building to keep pursuers' heads down. The others were getting sorted out in the arroyo behind him, lining out and drumming forward.

Provo went up past the protective shoulder of earth at a dead run and held the horse to that straining uphill gait for a quarter of a mile. He reined in to blow the horse, out of breath himself and streaming sweat.

The others came up and brought their horses to precipitate halts that spewed dust.

Portugee bawled, 'What the hell — no money?'

Menendez said, 'Maybe a few honnerd.'

'Shit.'

'Never mind,' George Weed said. 'We just lost a gamble, that's all. Shut up your whining, Portugee, you starting to sound too much like old Lee Roy.'

'I ain't Lee Roy and you better remember it. Nobody's gonna get to me that easy, Menendez.'

'Nobody's planning to,' Menendez said mildly.

Provo said, 'Shut up. Listen – we need to move. We work north around that hogback there, quiet and easy, we don't want anybody hearing us. Let the fools think we faded back into the mountains west. Come on — easy does it. Taco, hang on to Lee Roy's horse, we're going to need it.'

He lifted his reins and put the horse forward, a clambering single-foot with the horse's head bobbing in effort, crossing uneven rocky ground.

The clothes were matted to Provo's back and he felt a bilious rage. Somebody had persuaded that paymaster, and most likely every other cashier in town, to leave their money in the bank today. No hick sheriff would have thought of that. It had to be Burgade. Burgade was like that: unhurried, methodical, thorough, prepared for all the possibilities.

Menendez kicked his horse up alongside. 'Who's the spare horse for, Zach?' It was a question but Menendez spoke it flat, as a demand.

'Burgade set this up against us,' Provo said. 'Time to start knocking Burgade down.'

'The horse is for *Burgade*?'

'Not hardly,' Provo said, and flicked a thin smile at him.

They worked their way wide around and headed back down towards Tucson. Crossing the Santa Cruz they picked up Will Gant where he was waiting by the severed telephone wires. The six of them trotted up the riverbank in the trees, past the quiet old quarter of town. If anyone noticed them there was no alarm. Sunlight filtered down through the treetops, dappling the ground. Behind the bulk of a freight warehouse Provo called a brief halt.

'I'll take Will and the spare horse. Menendez, you take the rest of them on up to the Rillito and cut for Rose Canyon. Shelby and Quesada ought to be back there by now. Hole up and wait for us — we'll be along directly.'

'What the hell you op to, Zach?'

'You'll see. On the run, now.' He leaned out of the saddle to pick up the reins of Lee Roy's riderless horse from Taco.

Will Gant pulled off the track and let the others ride by. Provo waited until Menendez had taken them north out of sight in the trees; then he said to Gant, 'Just back my play, Will, this won't take but a minute.'

Gant grunted incuriously and adjusted his great bulk on his saddle. Provo turned right past the warehouse and rode past freight corrals and a mechanics' shop and on through a district of adobe shacks towards the big trees of the old residential district. He knew the route as if a map were engraved on his eyelids. They passed a few pedestrians who glanced at them and noticed nothing amiss and went on about their business.

North on Main Street and east on Third, left on Meyer Avenue, around past the old McKinney place and on to the quiet tree-shady street. His pulse started to pound when he drew rein in front of the house. 'Step down and hold these horses, will you? I'll be right out.'

'Nice and peaceful here, ain't it, Zach?'

'Sure is,' he said, feeling grim and jumpy. He walked up the tile-bordered walk to the screen door, trying to look calm and businesslike. Rapped the brass door-knocker and saw movement through the screen. He put one hand inside his duster through the slot pocket and drew his revolver, holding it down against his leg, concealed by the coat.

She came to the door drying her hands on a towel. A stray lock of brown hair had fallen across her face from under her sun-bonnet; she tossed it back with a shake of her head. She was a tall girl in a homespun dress. Provo's eyes followed the lines of her body as she approached the screen door. Provo put a polite smile on his face.

She stood just inside the door. 'Yes?'

'Miss Susan Burgade?'

'Yes,' she said, puzzled.

'Your daddy asked me to come over, make sure you're all right. Expecting some hard cases in town this morning, you know.'

'Yes, I know,' she said, not altogether sure of him. 'I did

hear something a little while ago. Is my father all right?'

'He's fine, ma'am. You mean that explosion — doing some blasting up to the smelter, I think. Nothing to fret yourself about. Look, ma'am, you mind if I come inside? Your daddy asked me to keep an eye on you until this business is over with. You never know what those hard cases might try.'

She didn't open the door. 'I'm afraid I don't know you.'

He didn't want to show his gun out here in broad daylight. He gave her a broader smile and tipped his hat back with his left hand. 'I just come down to help out with this trap of his. Sam and me go back a long way together — I worked for him back when he was heading up the railroad's security branch. Name of Carlos O'Neill, maybe you heard him mention me.'

'I can't say I have,' she said, and unlatched the door hesitantly. 'But I'm sure it must be all right. I'm sorry to seem to standoffish, Mr. O'Neill, but this whole thing troubles me, you know — I'm worried about my father, he shouldn't have involved himself in all this. He's not young.'

'Oh, I reckon Sam can always take care of himself,' he said, pulling the screen door open and stepping inside with his smile.

As soon as the door flapped shut behind him he showed her the gun. The smile dropped off his face as totally as if it had never been there: as if he were an actor, stepping backstage into the wings, shedding his role.

'All right, missy,' he said in a more abrasive voice than he'd used before. 'Now just keep quiet and listen to me.'

Fear quivered in her eyes. She backed up against the wall; her hand went to her mouth. 'What is it — what do you want?' It was a tiny whisper.

A faint miasmic breeze came in through the screen, stirring the tails of his duster around his legs. 'Let's go back to your room, missy, wherever you keep your things. You'll be needing some clothes — you're going on a little horseback trip with us.'

Stunned, she stood back in the bedroom corner, hugging

her breasts, staring at him without blinking, too unsettled to move. Provo flung open drawers and the wardrobe, found a carpetbag valise and opened it and put it on the bed. 'Come on, missy, I don't know what sort of things you need. You pack it yourself.'

She shook her head, mute. There was a thread of moisture on her upper lip. Her face, which had flooded with colour in the beginning, had gone unnaturally pale. Her eyes were very large.

He took two strides and cuffed her hard across the cheek. It rocked her head to one side and left red fingermarks. She reached up with one hand to touch her cheek; she blinked and drew a ragged breath. 'You — you're Provo.'

'That's right, missy.'

'Oh, my God,' she whispered, staring at him.

'Time's wasting,' he said. 'I don't want to hit you again.' He pointed his gun towards the open valise.

Moving like a sleepwalker, she crossed the room to the chest of drawers and began taking things out without discrimination and throwing them in the valise. She went to the wardrobe and took down denim trousers and a shirt and stuffed them in on top. Provo saw an oilskin rain slicker hanging inside and reached for it. 'Better take this along too.'

When she seemed done, he buckled the valise shut and carried it into the front of the house, prodding the girl ahead of him. 'Sit down at the table over there and write me a note for your old man.'

Her face came around, hollow and pallid. 'What?'

'We wouldn't want him to fret about you, would we? He might get all het up if he came home and you weren't anywhere around and he didn't know where you'd gone. Now you just sit down there and write him a little note. Tell him you've gone away with Zach Provo.'

'Gone — gone away where?'

'I guess he doesn't need to know that, does he, missy?' He shoved her towards the inkstand.

She still wore her sunbonnet — she must have been out

hanging wash on the line. She looked little-girlish when she sat down hesitantly and reached for the pen, dipped it into the inkwell and poised it above a sheet of paper. 'I — '

'I don't care what you tell him, missy, but write something.' He smiled slightly: 'I ain't illiterate, if it matters. I'll want to read what you've written. But it doesn't matter what you say. Go ahead now.'

The nib of the pen scratched across the paper in jerky squeaks. The silence began to unnerve Provo and he stepped forward to read over the girl's shoulder. She shrank away from him but continued writing until she had filled most of the sheet. Then tears began to drip from her eyes, blurring the writing, and Provo took the pen out of her hand and gripped her by the elbow. 'That's enough. We're leaving now.'

'Please,' she whispered. 'Please, I beg you, don't — '

He steered her towards the door, professing not to have heard her. When they reached the screen he stopped her. 'I've got this gun in my hand under my coat, missy, and there's a big man out at the kerb by the name of Will Gant, a good dear friend of mine. You try to bolt for it and one of us'll put a bullet in your leg, hear? Now you just walk out there right in front of me and climb on that horse and ride out of town between us, and there won't be any trouble. Nobody means to hurt you, just remember that. I just mean to make your old man sweat awhile and use you for a hostage to make sure we get safe conduct out of this bailiwick. You hear me, missy?'

She nodded and swallowed.

He squeezed her arm. 'Say it, missy. Say you hear me and you understand me and you ain't going to act foolish.'

'I understand,' she said weakly.

He tightened his grip on her valise, showed her the gun, slipped it back under his coat and nodded to her. She opened the screen door and stepped outside.

He stayed close behind her down the walk. Will Gant stood watching, burly and muscular, thighs bulging against his trousers. His eyes frankly coveted the girl's body but

Gant said nothing that might have displayed surprise. Provo said, 'Meet Miss Burgade, Will. She's going to side with us a way.'

Gant smiled and tugged at a black nostril hair. His thick lips peeled back. 'Pleased to make your acquaintance, ma'am.'

'Climb aboard, missy. Time to go.'

CHAPTER FOUR

CARRYING the tearstained note, Sam Burgade went, as if against his will, into his daughter's room. It was sunny in there, the muslin curtains stirring in a warm breeze, womanly things scattered around in disarray, drawers flung open, the wardrobe standing ajar.

Burgade's face kept changing. Muscles stood ridged at his jaw hinges and the bones at brow and cheek became harder, more prominent.

He pushed his solemn glance at things in the room as if to engrave them indelibly on his memory. Then he strode out of the house and marched, not running, around half the block to Packer's little grocery. Packer had a telephone. Burgade got through to the sheriff's office.

Noel Nye's voice came at him, scratchy and distant. 'Oh, there you are. Listen, that big noise from up on the hills, it was them. They blowed up the smelter safe. Left one of their own dead behind — one of my boys recognised him, Lee Roy Tucker. It was them convicts, all rat. They tooken off with a coupla hundred dollars petty caish.'

'That's not all they've taken,' Burgade said. 'Susan's gone.'

Nye came into the house wiping his face on his shirt-sleeve. His face in all its clubbed ugliness was full of forlorn dignity. 'Captain, I cain't tell you how sorry I am.'

'Yeah.' Burgade's scalp contracted.

'Well, de doin' everthang we can to get her back, Captain. Everybody owns a horse and a gun's out there beatin' the brush for sign.'

'Out where?'

The sheriff spread his hands. 'Mostly up in the mountains back of the smelter.'

'They didn't go that way. They had to come by here to collect my daughter. They didn't have her with them when they robbed the smelter, did they? Well, then — they must have come this way. From here they could only head up the valley towards Phoenix or up into the Catalinas.'

'Sure, Captain, you're rat. Too much goin' on rat now, I reckon — I ain't been thanking straight. Hell, I better not set around here and jaw all day.' He clapped on his campaign hat and swung to the door.

'I'm coming with you.'

'But — '

'She's my daughter, Noel.'

'Sure enough. Hell, come on, then.'

At noon a council of war was held in the sheriff's office. Reports came in by telephone from the edges of the city. Nothing came in from beyond the town limits; the cross-country wires were down somewhere, doubtless cut by Provo's men. It might take the linemen a day to find the breaks and repair them.

'In the meantime,' Sheriff Nye said judiciously, 'let's sort out what we do know. They's probably eight of them. Five men was seen at the smelter office but one's dead, Tucker. That's four, and one to hold the horses makes five. Sixth man down the road between the smelter and town to cut the telephone. Seventh and eighth at both ends of Tucson to cut the wares. All rats. We got to figure they all of 'em armed to the teeth. They cut crosst along the Rillito, I reckon, so they must of rendezvoused somewheres up in the foothills of the Catalinas. That's where most of our people are lookin' now. Captain, how do you tote it?'

Burgade was sitting towards the back of the room, dry-washing his hands. Heads swivelled towards him — the mayor, the chief of police, the undersheriff, the editor of the *Star*, three or four councilmen, the county supervisor, and the prosecuting attorney. They all watched him with grave concern.

'They're on horseback,' Burgade said slowly, weighing his

words. 'You can't hope to block off the roads and railroads and catch them that way. They've got to be tracked, the old way, by men on horseback. That's how I tote it.'

The mayor said, 'But is that wise, Sam? If they catch sign of pursuit won't it put Susan in danger?'

'She's in danger with them at all times,' Burgade said in a flat voice. 'They expect to be tracked. Provo's not a stupid man. He took my daughter because he wanted revenge against me — a personal thing. But he also took her because he wanted a hostage, and that means that wherever he's planning to go, he realises he won't be able to hide his back trail. If he planned to head directly into Mexico and hide out in the Sierras he'd have killed Susan by now — she'd only slow him down. No, he — '

'Wait, Sam,' the prosecuting attorney said. 'I don't know how to put this so it won't twist the knife. But how do we know they haven't already killed Susan?'

'They made her pack several changes of clothes.'

'Is that conclusive enough?'

'It is to me. Provo wants to keep her alive. He knows if we find her dead, nothing on earth will stop me from finding him and putting him to the most painful death it's possible for a man to have. No. She's alive. As long as she's alive with him, I bleed and he knows I'm bleeding and he also knows I've got to keep my distance.'

'The goddamned bastard's clever,' the mayor said. 'As clever a fiend as — '

'Let's not waste time calling him names.' Burgade's eyes were flinty, glittering, unfathomable: he kept his feelings strictly to himself. His voice was level, under total control. 'There's no reason why any of you should abide by my judgment any longer. I'm the one who created this disaster. I'm responsible for what's happened this morning — Susan wouldn't be gone and the smelter office wouldn't have been blown up if my scheme hadn't drawn Provo here. Replacing that vault will cost thousands — you might advise the manager that I'm prepared to make restitution to whatever limits my savings can cover. Now, as to the — '

'Nonsense,' the mayor exploded. 'You can't possibly be held to blame for the mindless animal savaging of these beasts. If anything, the smelter's in your debt — you advised them to postpone their payday, otherwise the vault would have been full of cash.'

'That's neither here nor there,' Burgade said. 'We're getting off the point. I don't have the power to insist that anybody heed my advice after what happened this morning, but what I'm going to do is provision myself with a horse and some weapons and get on Provo's track. I intend to stick to the track until I can get my daughter out of their hands and then I intend to kill Provo and his crew the way you'd kill a pack of rabid wolves. I'm speaking for myself. I'd be obliged for company but I've got no authority to ask for it.'

He put his hands on his knees and stood up slowly, feeling old in his joints, feeling as if a fist had slammed him low in the belly and crumpled him. Dry-eyed, he walked to the door.

He hired the best horse Ochoa had in the stable and a good solid double-rig saddle with plenty of concho strings and a leather rifle boot and a long skirt behind the cantle across which provisions could be strapped. He had to hold in the nervous prancing gelding on his way down the crowded streets; the horse danced along half-sideways. He tethered it to the gatepost in front of his house and went inside to make up a field pack for himself.

He chose each item with studied care. A lightweight rawhide rope, sixty feet long, coiled in a tight ring. A two-quart water canteen. Blanket-roll and rain slicker. Folding pocket knife and a nine-inch fighting knife in a leather scabbard slotted for threading over a gunbelt. Antiseptic and bandage cloth. A folding razor, not for whisker-shaving but for use as a weapon, a slicing blade, and a snakebite remedy. Gloves and a fleece-lined mackinaw for the high country, if the trail should take him that way. Flint-and-wheel fire-lighter and a waterproof oilskin pouch of sulphur matchsticks. His old Army-style mess kit, with its accordion-collapsible cooking pot and coffee cup, its mated locked cookpans and utensils. Soap, a spare shirt, underdrawers, socks, a thick soft pair of Hopi moccasins, a coil of strong fine fishing line, twine ball, towel, field glasses, steel picket stake, rope hobbles. He packed it all together with tight efficiency, most of it inside the blanket-roll and the rest in saddlebags which he left as empty as possible to accommodate food and ammunition.

He went into the front room and unlocked the gun chain. Took down the Springfield bolt-action ·30–06. He weighted the saddlebags down with ammunition and went outside carrying canteen, blanket-roll, saddlebags, and rifle. Stowed them all aboard the horse and climbed up into the saddle and rode at a trot around to Packer's grocery. He went inside and bought enough provisions, as concentrated as he could find, to fill a small gunnysack, which he tied on top of the blanket-roll with piggin' strings.

That was it, then. He couldn't think of anything he'd forgotten. He put his foot in the stirrup and gathered the reins and hoisted himself up. It was a stiff climb for an old man: he had to lift his right leg high over the pile of provisions. He got settled with half his weight on the balls of his feet in the wood stirrups, adjusted the reins in the fingers of his left hand, tugged his hatbrim down tight, and clucked to the horse.

Sheriff Nye came up the street with a mounted posse — young Hal Brickman, very graven-faced, and eight or nine deputies.

'Here you are,' Nye said. 'Thought we missed you back at the house.'

'Why,' Sam Burgade said, 'I'm obliged, Noel.'

'My job, ain't it, Captain?'

They found the camp in Rose Canyon at about four in the afternoon. There was no mistake about it because a bit of cloth clung to an obvious branch. It was torn off Susan's sunbonnet, the one she wore around the house on washday.

'Message from Zach Provo,' Burgade drawled. The surfaces of his eyes glittered like hard gems.

Nye said, 'They cain't have more than four, five hours' jump on us.' He turned back to his horse. 'Come on, the trail don't get no shorter while we set here staring at it.'

Burgade saw Hal Brickman's eyebrows contract. The young man was staring around the creek-bank camp ground with a grief-stricken look that was no sham; he had kept it to himself on the ride up from Tucson but he was beginning to look as if he was ready to let loose. He cut a faintly ludicrous figure in his narrow snap-brim hat and dude jodhpurs, a revolver buckled awkwardly around his waist, high up in one of those Army-style holsters with a protective snap-down flap. If he'd carried his gun inside his saddlebag it might have been a little harder to reach, but not much. Still, his earnest anger was genuine and he had not whimpered. In other circumstances, Burgade might have had a great deal of room for sympathy towards him: Hal's anguished face was evidence enough of the sincerity of his love for Susan and the agony of not knowing what he could do to save her.

Nye was down on one knee. 'Look here, Captain.'

Burgade went over to him and leaned over to focus his attention on the ground at the point of the sheriff's finger.

'One of them horses got a tie-bar shoe here, lakly to hold in a soft hoof.'

'That'll leave a distinctive print,' Burgade said. He walked forward leading his horse, seeing where the tie-bar track went. There was a big muddle of prints where several horses had trampled one another's tracks but towards the upper end of the clearing it got sorted out and Burgade turned back to gather his reins and climb into the saddle. 'They went on up the canyon.'

'Ain't trying hard to hide their tracks, that's for sure,' Nye said.

Hal Brickman brought his horse up to the head of the column. 'Look, I'm not sure about all this.'

Sun and wind wrinkles gathered at the corners of Burgade's eyes. 'Nobody is, Hal.'

'No, I mean won't they be likely to harm Susan if we crowd them?'

'They'll be more likely to harm her if we don't.'

'I'm sorry, sir, but that doesn't make much sense to me.'

Noel Nye said, 'Gentle down, son. This is just as hard on the Captain as it is on you. You got to trust us to know what we doing.'

Hal's tortured eyes swept from face to face. 'Look, you know all about manhunting and fighting and I'm just an engineer, I'm a greenhorn here, and I admit it. But I don't care about bringing these men to justice or getting revenge or anything else. I just want to try and help make sure Susan isn't hurt.'

'That's what we all want,' Nye said. 'Son, you bound to take our word for it, we know what we doing — the Captain knows what he's doing.'

Burgade's bleak glance simmered on the trees up-canyon. Hal spoke rapidly, his voice climbing, starting to lose control: 'If we push them they may get rattled — God knows what they may do. Suppose they panic? Suppose they split up and run for it? They won't leave Susan behind, alive.'

Burgade said, very mild, 'Then what do you suggest?'

'My God, I don't know, but shouldn't we take it easy?'

'And let them get clean away, you mean,' Nye said. 'What good's that going to do her?'

Burgade said, 'We're wasting time,' and put his horse up into the tress.

At the head of the canyon the tracks took them along the sloping side of a scrubby hogback and up towards the dip in the centre of a high-ground saddle. Burgade unsheathed his field glasses and played them over the higher stretches ahead. Magnification made the sun-struck pinpoints of mica reflections strike his eyes like needles. A dry layer of heat lay along the mountains; the slopes lifted steeply towards tall-timber country and timberline beyond, the bald ten-thousand-foot summits of the Catalinas. Along here it was mostly loose sun-whacked earth and boulders, bucking up towards the Windy Point district.

He didn't see any sign of movement but that was no surprise; the great shoulders of these mountains could hide — and had hidden — armies. The Chiricahua Apaches had fought a campaign up here, using the torturous canyon mazes as a stronghold againt Hitchcock's struggling troopers. Three decades ago Burgade had tracked renegade Indians and outlaw fugitives through this patch of the Rockies, and nothing had changed; the crags and gorges were as immutable as time. It was a stiff ankle-bursting climb to the passes, but once down the far side it was a fast level run up the flat bed of the San Pedro Valley towards the high pine country of central east Arizona and the lava badlands beyond, or the Apache and Navajo country to the south. Or, if Provo had turned south along the San Pedro, he would have an easy trail along the Southern Pacific Railroad spur to Bowie, from which he could disappear in any direction — east towards Lordsburg and El Paso, south through Cochise's old battlefields into Mexico, west into the chopped-up Huachuca country around Tombstone. Down in that lower right-hand corner of Arizona you could hide out for fifty years without being found, if you didn't mind the heat and the rocks and the total lack of greenery. Cochise and Geronimo had proved that. But Burgade had a feeling Provo wasn't going to turn that way.

The posse climbed steadily into the waning afternoon. There was no talk. Nobody knew what they were going to do if they did somehow catch up with the fugitives; nobody wanted to talk about that, except Hal Brickman, and Hal kept his own counsel after Burgade's rebuff.

Burgade had ideas how to handle it, but there was no point in spelling them out until the time came. In the meantime his old backside was starting to get saddlesore already and he concentrated his attention on the faint scuffmarks and dents of the fugitives' track.

Just on sunset they climbed out of a canyon thick with clawing manzinita and saw the juniper-piñon slopes rising ahead, northeast, while a swift grade fell away to the right towards the lower pass and Spud Rock in the Rincon peaks. The tie-bar print and its companion hooftracks arrowed straight up into the piñon forest. Nye crowded his horse up alongside Burgade and said, 'Could be they trying to throw us off here. If I was them I'd head down that slope over the easy pass instead of goin' over the top the hard way. What you bet they done cut off up ahead and doubled back down over Redington way?'

'No,' Burgade said, 'they're headed over the top.'

'Well, Captain, I ain't so sure about that. And the light's gettin' poor for tracking. No use trailin' blind — we better camp here and track at sunup.'

'Camp if you want to. I'm going on. Provo won't stop tonight — I don't want to give him an extra eight hours on us.'

'Maybe you're rat. But if they turn off someplace during the night, we gonna lose more'n eight hours, time we back-track and pick up the trail again. You fixin' to take that chance?'

'I am.'

'You always was a gambler.'

'I think I know where he's headed, Noel, and I mean to catch him before he gets there.'

'Where's that?'

'Window Rock Reservation.'

Nye's eyes widened. 'All the way up there? Hell, our people in Tucson ought to have the telephone and telegraph wares fixed up by now, Captain. Posses gonna be deploying out of every town between here and Window Rock — and that's two hundred mile. Provo'd be a fool to run that gantlet.'

'He'd be a bigger fool not to. He's got a hostage, remember? No posse's going to brace him. He'll stay out of their way if he can, but if they jump him they'll have to give him room to get by. He's counting on that, otherwise he'd have been covering his tracks by now.'

'All rat, then, since you brang it up. Suppose we do get close to him. What then?'

'Let's catch him first,' Burgade said, and put his horse up into the piñons.

CHAPTER FIVE

WHEN the leader called a halt, Susan dismounted, moving awkwardly, uncomfortably conscious of her body and the way some of them stared at her. She was still in a detached state, like a waking dream — everything she saw registered on her mind, she was aware of every detail, but she felt stunned. Very little anger had seeped through the haze, and not much fear.

While Zach Provo walked a few paces out on to a promontory slab and extended his collapsible spyglass, the rest of them stood around dividing up a small sheaf of money. From the talk, she gathered they had stolen it from the smelter. She watched the young one wad up his folded greenbacks and insert them in a chamber of his six-gun 'Rainyday money,' he said drily, looking at the cloudless twilit sky. The sun had just gone down with a blaze and a wink.

The young one had a friendly face. His name was Mike Shelby; he had told her cheerfully on the trail. *Why don't we just abandon convention and introduce ourselves?* He seemed incredibly easygoing, as if nothing really touched him. She envied him: she knew that soon she was going to wake up to the unspeakable terror of it.

As though it were a social Sunday picnic the young Shelby had named all of them for her. Somehow the names had lodged; it was a habit she had developed on purpose as a schoolteacher. Each term on the first day of class she asked each new student his name, and had a way of fixing her stare on the pupil's face so as to memorise it and associate the name with it. Dear Lord, that classroom was in another world.

The sky was red to the west. The little one, Cesar Menendez, had walked out on to the point of rock with Provo and she heard Provo's toneless voice. 'Coming right along.' Provo lowered the telescope and pushed it shut.

Menendez said, 'Burgade with them?'

'Too far away to tell. But he's got to be. Wild horses couldn't hold the bastard back.' Provo turned on his heel and came back towards them. His cold stare flicked across Susan; for a moment she closed her eyes, trying to shut it all out, but a twanging voice which she identified as Portugee Shiraz's said, 'I got to take a leak.' She opened her eyes and saw Portugee, unbuttoning his fly, walk off into the rocks, the bad teeth showing in his vulpine face. His skin was dark as George Weed's but his features were not as heavily Negroid. They were a strange admixture of races, these convicts — only two of them, Will Gant and young Mike Shelby, were (or at least appeared to be) white men; Provo had a leathery Indian face, Portugee Shiraz was at least part black, George Weed was the colour of a charred steak, Taco Riva appeared to be Mexican-Indian, Menendez of the same stock, and the silent Joaquim Quesada, big-faced and half bald, probably had as much *mestizo* blood as Spanish *conquistador* in him.

In some way, keeping them all sorted out this way seemed a necessary exercise in the preservation of sanity. Identifying them by colour and cheekbone-shape was an arbitrary way to classify them but it kept her brain busy; as she heard them speak more, she would start sorting them out by personality and talents . . . What was this madness? They weren't fourth-grade pupils! *You have got to get a grip on yourself.*

When Portugee came back she saw Zach Provo pick up the reins of his horse. 'Mount up.'

'Aw, Jesus, Zach,' said Portugee, 'I'm tard.'

'Posse down there,' Menendez told him in a casual way. 'You want to es-sleep till they get here and arres' you, Portugee?'

'Hell, they got to keep their distance long as we got her.'

'Don't count on it,' said Will Gant, and came around from the far side of his horse to face Portugee and Zach Provo.

Portugee said, 'Then what'd we brang her for?'

'Because Zach wants to sweat old Sam Burgade.'

Portugee scowled and bit a hangnail on his thumb. She saw Mike Shelby turn to watch the byplay. Will Grant said, 'Time we got one or two thangs straight, Zach.'

'No time for that now.'

Mike Shelby said, 'Maybe let him get it off his chest. He's lookin' as unhappy as a soaked cat.' He smiled in a friendly way. Quesada looked on, mute; Taco Riva was holding his horse by the bit chains, murmuring to it, indifferent to the others.

Will Gant shifted his stance. He seemed to realise he had thrown raw meat on the ground. He cleared his throat and said irresolutely, 'Look, all I mean is, we come all the way down here on Zach's say-so to git us a heap of money, and what'd we end up with? A few dollars pocket change. All's we want now is get shet of that posse. Maybe as long as we hang on to this girl we keep them at arm's length, but ain't nothing stopping them from tracking us, don't matter where we go. We can't hide out with them ten mile behint us. We keep going like this and sooner or later they going to nail us, girl or no girl. We can't all stand in a line behint her when the bullets start flying. What I say, we ought to split up soon as we get acrosst these mountains. Everybody go their own way. Posse can't chase all of us if we all go different ways.'

Provo said, 'You're talking out of turn, Will.'

'No. You ain't my warden, Zach. Look, you want to get Sam Burgade hogtied and sweatin', that's your lookout. But we ain't forgetting Sam Burgade would like to see you right where you'd like to see him. You was born to get hung, Zach, and I don't rightly see no reason why the rest of us got to get hung alongside of you. You go ahead and play out your string with Burgade, that's your business, ain't nobody trying to stop you. But I don't cotton to it myself. I'm fixin' to go my own way once we over the top.'

'You're wasting wind,' Provo said. 'Are you fool enough to think that's the only posse in Arizona? By now they've got those cross-country wires spliced together and they've sent word on us out to every hick town in the state. I'm the only thing in the world that's keeping you out of their hands, Will — me and missy, here. You go busting off on your own and they'll hunt you down in no time flat.'

'I guess I'll just take that chance.'

Susan glanced towards Menendez. His sharp little face was watchful and immobile. She looked away, chilled, and plucked at the frayed seams of her ripped sunbonnet. Provo had ripped a big piece of it off to hang on a twig down in Rose Canyon where her father couldn't miss seeing it. *Poisoned,* she thought — *His mind's poisoned.* She was beginning to wake up, she realized; her body was going rigid, starting to tremble.

Portugee said in his high-pitched twang, 'He's rat, Zach. No hard feelings, now, but you got us this far on yo' promise that we was gonna get a lot of money out of that smelter. Maybe it wasn't yo' fault, maybe lak you said it was Burgade put them up to it, but all the same we just as broke as we was before. I reckon I got as good a chance my own self as I got stickin' with you-all.'

'No,' Provo said. 'We stay together. All of us.'

Will Gant moved wider away from Portugee, snapped a glance at Menendez, and said, 'What the hell for, Zach? Why you so damn set on keepin' us together?'

'It's for your own good, Will.' But even to Susan it sounded lame; she looked at Provo in bewilderment. She saw his eyes flicker, shifting from face to face, and knew what he was doing — he was measuring each one of them, sizing them up. Probably trying to decide how many were on his side. She hadn't sorted out all their loyalties and knew nothing of their motives, but it was clear that for whatever reason, Menendez was Provo's ally. As for the rest, it was impossible for her to tell. She had a feeling Shelby was willing to go along with Provo, but not to the extent of fighting the others over it. Taco Riva didn't seem to care about much of anything except the horses. Quesada was unfathomable. George Weed had not spoken ten words in her hearing and she had no idea of his sentiments — until now, when Weed stirred and spoke:

'Maybe you better spell out whatever it is you got in mind, Zach. Then we can decide.'

Provo seemed indignant. 'I've pulled all of you through this far, haven't I? You know what happened to the rest of the cons that busted out with us, don't you? Every one of them ended up back in Yuma. All except you men — because I took you under my wing. You're still loose because I'm the only one with brains enough to keep you loose. And you want to walk out on me. All right, walk. See how far you get.' He wheeled in his horse in anger and gathered the reins to mount.

It was Quesada, strangely, who spoke: 'That's not enough any more, Zach.'

It turned Provo around. 'What?'

The big bald-headed man had a slow, apologetic way of talking. He looked like a drunk, with his purplish face and big red nose and shifty eyes. 'You had a plan, before. We was gonna get enough money to get out of the country. Like Portugee said, maybe it wasn't your fault the money wasn't there. But at least we had it to shoot for. What we got to shoot for now? What are you offering us?'

Provo snorted. 'Your skins.'

'Maybe we can look out after our own skins, Zach.'

'Maybe you just think you can.' But he was looking them over again and Susan could see it when he realised he had lost them. Weed, Portugee, Gant, Quesada, they had all turned cold towards him. Shelby was frowning at his boots, not sure which way to turn. Menendez was the only one who didn't look worried and adamant. Even Taco Riva was watching with evident interest.

Provo let the reins drop from his fist and turned away from his horse to face the rest of them. He looked slightly disgusted. For a moment his hard stare rested against Susan and she felt the icy touch of dread.

Provo said, 'It's like this. I owe Sam Burgade. I owe him a little something for the twenty-eight years I put in on the rockpile and for one or two other things we don't need to go into. I want you gents to help me pay off that debt. No, let me finish. You want to know what's in it for you. I'll tell you. First, where I'm taking you, that posse won't be able to follow us. It's out of bounds for them. Burgade, maybe, but Burgade's just one man. The posse won't come with him. Figure out those odds and then stack them up against the odds you'd face if you cut out on me and tried to run for it on your own with every sheriff in Arizona looking to nail you. Second, you still want money. All right. I've got forty-eight thousand dollars in gold coin buried up on the Mogollon Rim. I need to use some of it to pay off certain people to make sure the law ain't allowed to follow us where we're going. I intend to keep some of it for myself. But I'll put up twenty-one thousand dollars. It's yours to split — three thousands apiece. Three thousand dollars is a lot of money to a man on the run. Now let's get on these horses and move out. You think about my offer on the way over the top.'

He turned quickly, breaking up the tableau. 'Come on, missy, put it in the saddle, all right? Or do I have to pick you up and tie you on?'

Riva rode point, because he seemed able to communicate things to a horse that nobody else could. Riva picked the path in the starlit dark, and the rest followed at a steady slow-climbing pace. Susan sat her saddle loosely, weary, resting both hands on the saddle horn because she didn't have reins to hold — Quesada had the reins, he was leading her horse. They weren't taking any chances with her. Provo had tied one of her ankles to the stirrup leathers to ensure she wouldn't try to jump off her horse and run for it in the darkness. She had bent down once to try and shift the knot, because it was digging her ankle bone painfully, but the man right behind her – Menendez – had spoken sharply and gigged his horse close and threatened to slash her with his quirt, and she had straightened up and ridden in silence after that.

She felt grit-dirty inside the homespun dress. It seemed clear that Provo intended to push straight through the night, only stopping now and then to breathe the horses. At this rate she wondered how long he expected the animals to last, let alone their riders.

Through the first few hours of the night ride she swung from mood to mood like a lunatic, weaving from one extreme of emotion to another: terrorised dread that made her tremble violently and repress screams of fear; furious rages that made her want to claw the eyes out of all their faces — she had wild violent visions of tying them all to stakes and building huge fires around them — and left her weak, drained; dirges of self-pitying resignation, waiting for them to kill her and be done with it; frightful fantasies in which she saw them holding her down, spreadeagling her, venting their sweaty lusts upon her body; spates of cynical uncaring exhaustion in which she went numb, told herself to just mark time until it was over — hope to survive it, and ignore whatever might happen in the meantime.

Finally they reached the summit of the pass and started down the long eastward slope towards the San Pedro River. It must have been well past midnight, although she was not versed in reading the time by stars. Her body was slack, moving loosely with the jolts and shifts of the saddle. The hot rages and icy terrors had cooled and thawed within her; fantasies had dulled, resolve had dissipated. It was no longer necessary to force indifference upon herself. She was too washed-out to care any more. She swayed as if she were asleep; she was not asleep, but neither was she altogether awake. A kind of peace had settled on her, a protective daze from which she did not expect, or want, to emerge.

The first shadow-streaks of dawn caught them in the foothills, still heading for the river. They were not hurrying the pace but they had kept moving steadily, eating up ground. Someone rode by and passed her a cold hard biscuit and a strip of dried beef, and when she had eaten them she looked up and saw it was Mike Shelby, watching her gravely, holding his horse alongside hers. He handed her a canteen and she drank from it greedily. She didn't think to hand it back to him, and he took it gently out of her grasp, capped it and slung it over his saddle horn. He seemed to smile a little in the dawn, and then he dropped back towards the tail end of the column.

Daylight grew steadily; it seemed to revive some of them. Portugee Shiraz pulled up beside her and said, 'You want some grub, lassie?'

Menendez, behind her, said, 'Shelby already fed her.'

'Tryin' to get the inside track,' Portugee said, and cackled unpleasantly. 'Well, that's all rat, I reckon maybe we all get a turn at you 'fore this is over, lassie. Soon as we get time to stop awhile. Hey, Menendez, she's a real looker, this'n. I like the tits on her.'

'Turn them upside down, they all the es-same,' Menendez replied with Mexican indifference to cruelty.

Portugee gave a bray of laughter. 'Look, she's sweating,' he said, pleased. 'We got her scared. You scared, lassie? Scared maybe we gonna mo-lest you? Haw!'

'Wouldn't want to get her upset,' Menendez said. 'She might wet her pants.'

'Aw, naw, we wouldn't want that. Now you just take it easy now, lassie. Don't fret yo'seff none.' To Menendez he added, 'I always say, a contented cow gives the sweetest milk.'

From up ahead of Quesada, Provo's voice came floating back: 'Shut up back there. Leave her alone.'

She had kept her eyes shut; she kept them shut now. She didn't know why Provo had any interest in protecting her from the rest of them but whatever his motive she was remotely glad of it.

Provo called a halt in the greasewood at the edge of the hardpan flats. Out across the valley she could see the dark ribbon of greenery that marked the course of the river. There was a tall structure of some kind, made of metal that glittered in the early sun. Probably a windmill, its blades flashing the reflections.

Provo pointed at it. 'That ought to be Vestal's horse ranch. We'll ride in and swap for fresh animals. Anybody puts an argument, show some iron — but don't kill anybody unless we have to. I ain't a butcher.'

She saw him look around at the rest of them. 'You've had all night to think on my offer. What about it? George?'

George Weed said, 'I could use three thousand. But where's this place where the law can't get after us?'

'Redrock country,' Provo told him. 'My people's place. Arizona law got no jurisdiction there.'

'Maybe — but who says those Navajos will let us come in?'

'As long as you're with me, they'll let you stay.' Provo's glance moved on. 'Portugee?'

'I guess,'

'Quesada? Will?'

Nobody said no.

'Let's go, then.'

CHAPTER SIX

THE sun burned everywhere it struck and the air was like coarse wool, so hot it was hard to breathe, and the dust was in Sam Burgade's teeth. Sunday, late afternoon: the heat lay in an intense shimmering layer along the high plateau, and dust devils funnelled erratically in yellow wheelings of sand, twigs, and leaves.

Burgade's eyes were raw with fatigue. He was filled with the agony of muscles that cried out from punishment after long disuse. He pulled up his dirt-caked horse on the hillside and tasted the posse's dust and unslung his field glasses for perhaps the thousandth time.

Down across the shallow bowl, past a fringe of scrubby trees, there was a sun-scraped ranch house. It had been painted, probably less than two years ago, but the ravenous sun had bleached all colour out of it. The field glasses brought it up close and clear: the eaves hung with cobwebs and the man who sat on the porch was as filthy and ramshackle as the place itself — a gaunt grey-stubbled figure in a black clawhammer coat, dusty and drab and shiny from long years of wearing. The man had one leg bandaged and propped up on a small wooden crate; a bottle of whisky hung in one clawed grey hand.

'The tracks go down there,' said Sheriff Nye.

'So do we,' Burgade said, and put his horse forward.

The old-timer on the porch had veinshot eyes. He spat tobacco juice off the porch and waited for the posse to come in. Then his face changed and he said, 'If it ain't Sam Burgade.'

Burgade tried to make out the features in the porch shade. The old man cackled: 'Shit, Sam, you don't recognise me.'

'Rinehart. Dutch Rinehart.'

'Sure I am.'

It was beyond belief. This old caved-in wreckage of a man. Burgade remembered him: full of spit and beans, top horse-wrangler on the Hatchet ranch. Burgade wiped a hand across his face to conceal his awe and the dismal rage of knowing he was himself just as old and used-up as the half-drunk human carrion on the porch.

Burgade was looking at the bandage wrapped unsanitarily around the spindly old leg. The old man was a strange sight in clawhammer coat and dirty white drawers, no trousers. 'You all right, Dutch?'

'Ain't but a bullet hole. Went through me clean. I've had worse.' The bleary eyes surveyed the posse. 'Shit, you still in the man-tracking business, Sam?'

'Looking for Zach Provo, Dutch.'

'I didn't get their names,' the old man said dryly. 'They was eight or nine of 'em. Scairt the pants off me, as you can plainly see.'

Sheriff Nye said, 'It was them shot you?'

'Yair, I sure as hell don't go round shootin' myself.'

'Why'd they do it?'

'I guess to keep me from walkin' into Snowflake and telling the law they was here,' Rinehart said, with an amazing lack of rancor. 'I only had but six or seven head of horses here but they tooken off with 'em all. You catch 'em, Sam, I'd be obliged if you get me my horses back.'

Burgade had climbed down; he walked up on to the porch and said, 'Better let me have a look at that, Dutch.'

'No, never mind. If you happen to ride through Snowflake you might ask Doc Travis to drop out here.' Rinehart waved him away. 'Shit, I'm all right. Take more'n a forty-five-calibre hole in the leg to do me much damage. It went clear through — bullet's in that wall over there. I stuck a hot running-iron through it. Cauterised up fine.'

Behind him, Burgade heard young Hal Brickman whisper an oath in amazed horror. It made Dutch Rinehart grin. 'These young ones ain't got no i-dee what tough is, do they, Sam?'

Burgade's face had closed up right. He said in a taut hoarse-weary voice, 'They had a girl with them.'

'Yair. Sure was a looker.'

'Was she all right, Dutch?' Burgade had to lick his dry, cracked lips.

'I guess. Hell, she was alive. She didn't look as if she cared much if she was alive or dead. Like she just didn't give a shit either way. But I guess she was all right. Why?'

'She's my daughter.'

'Oh, Jesus. Oh, Christ, Sam, I am sorry.'

'How long were they here?'

'Long enough to rope out all my horses. Listen, you get your hands on them, my Rocking Chair brand ain't hard to pick out. I'd be obliged.'

'How much of a jump have they got on us?'

'Six, maybe seven hours.' Rinehart spat an amber stream at the ground. His lips peeled back in a mostly toothless smile. 'They the toughest bunch I seen in a good spell. That skinny little Mex didn't bat an eye when he shot me. Just took aim, casual like, as if I was a tin can for practice. I swear I didn't really think he was gonna do anything until the damn gun went off. He wasn't even mad. Jesus, I'm sorry about your girl, Sam. I hope you run them down.'

'I will,' Burgade said. 'Thanks for your time, Dutch.'

'Hell, I wisht you could set a spell. You and me ain't jawed in years, we got a lot of catching up to do.'

'Take care of yourself. We'll send the doctor out.' Burgade went to his horse and climbed up, anguish in all his joints. He turned the horse and heard Nye say behind him, 'One little thang, Mr. Rinehart — you happened to notice which way they headed?' Nye's voice was dry and Burgade didn't miss the implied rebuke. *Getting rattled*, he admitted to himself, but he kept right on going and barely heard Rinehart's reply:

'Northeast. You want to watch out for them hard cases, mister, they don't — '

Burgade rode out of earshot. Past the deputies and Hal Brickman with his sunburnt, bleak, tired face, and kept on riding, not waiting for the others, angling out to the northeast and scanning the ground for sign. There was an urgency in him and Nye remarked it when he galloped up: 'Easy, Captain, let's don't windbreak these horses.'

'Another day and they'll be across the line, Noel.'

'Then let's get ourselves on into Snowflake and make a few telephone calls, get a couple of posses moving out of Winslow and Holbrook to head them off this side of the line.'

But the phones were dead in Snowflake, as might have been expected: the wires had been cut outside the town at both ends. They despatched the doctor to Rinehart's and rode on into the dusk.

They had been fifty-six hours on the trail now. Time and heat and jurisdictional boundaries had pared the posse down and changed the personnel: only one of Nye's deputies was still with them; the rest had gone back to Pima County to be replaced by men from Coconino and Navajo counties. Posses were out all over northeastern Arizona, New Mexico had squads combing the badlands, both Utah and Colorado had statewide alarms out. But it was a big wilderness. Provo had slipped through, cutting every wire he came across. The fugitives had avoided most towns and main roads; they had raided horse ranches frequently enough to keep supplied with fast mounts, and if they were sleeping at all they were doing it in the saddle, on the move.

The moon came up, a horned crescent not yet in its first quarter, only a thin rind; but there were no clouds and the starlight was good enough for tracking. Until they got into the chopped-up rocklands. Here it was all shale and petrified wood and there wasn't a chance of picking up sign at night. Nye started to curse. 'Christ, we know they're headed north, but northeast or northwest now? That line's two hundred mile long. They can cross it anyplace.'

'Provo had it planned out this way,' Burgade said. 'That's why he hasn't covered his tracks before. He knew he'd lose us along here.'

'Bastard,' Nye gritted.

'Let's get on into Holbrook.'

It was after midnight when they pulled into Holbrook and rode across the Santa Fe tracks. Huge grey moths rustled around the street lamps. The town was asleep. Burgade dismounted in agony and went into the sheriff's office. The place was awake because of the manhunt but the only two people in it were temporary deputies; the permanent staff was out combing the badlands somewhere. Burgade borrowed the telephone and tried to get through to Gallup and Winslow. The line to Winslow was dead, but he reached the telephone exchange in Gallup, which was just over the line in New Mexico, and after some discussion with the switchboard lady in Gallup he finally got a sleepy-voiced deputy U.S. marshall on the line. Burgade identified himself and explained the situation in three or four terse sentences and said, 'We'd take it kindly if you'd get on up to Window Rock, Marshal, and try to talk the Tribal Council into giving us permission to come aboard the Reservation to hunt these men down.'

When he concluded the call he went outside with Nye and propped his shoulder against the front of the building. He was too tired to stand up without support. He said, 'They cut the lines somewhere between here and Winslow. That's only a thirty-five mile stretch, so we've got a fair idea where they went across the Santa Fe tracks. It's my guess they crossed over close to the east end of Winslow. Two or three big outfits right around there where they might pick up fresh horses and provisions. From there, on a horseback guess, I'd say they'd go north along the Little Colorado as far as Corn Creek and head into the rough country from there.'

'That's prob'ly as good a guess as any,' Nye said. 'But it don't make no never-mind now, does it? They bound to be across the line by morning. We ain't gonna catch them now. Ain't got a prayer.'

'Maybe. Let's go down to the railroad depot.'

'Now that's an idea.'

They commandeered a switching engine and caboose and left their horses behind; they piled into the caboose with their saddles and kit. Burgade stretched out on a trainman's bunk and went immediately and thoroughly to sleep. Less than an hour later someone shook him awake. He came pawing up out of his coma like a man fighting an ocean undertow. Nye said, 'The boys scared us up some horses.'

'What time is it?'

'Little after two.'

'We've still got a chance, then. We must have picked up four or five hours on them.'

'Don't count on nothing, Captain — don't be gettin' yo' hopes up.'

Winslow town was dead asleep. Burgade stepped down off the caboose and saw Hal Brickman waiting with a pair of horses. Everybody else was already mounted. It registered fuzzily on Burgade's brain that the waiting horse was already cinched-up and ready to ride. Somebody had saddled up for him; they had let him sleep the extra minutes. It made him spiteful: he didn't want to be humoured or pampered. He climbed aboard, compressing his lips and gamely swinging his leg over, trying not to let them see how close he came to not making it.

He tugged his hat down. 'Somebody's missing.'

'Deppity Wellard,' Nye said. 'Provo turned loose of those horses he stole off your frind Rinehart. I told Wellard he could take the horses on back to Rinehart's and then go on home — he was pret' near played out anyhow. For that matter ain't none of us in no fit shape for this, Captain. I'm only statin' a fact. We ain't quitting.'

'Where'd they find Rinehart's horses?'

'Just outside the ranch over there where we hired these. Nobody seen them swap horses but they must of done it not more'n two, three hours ago. Yeah, you was rat — they did come by here.' Quiet respect echoed in Nye's voice.

Settling his stirrups, Burgade caught Hal Brickman's worried glance. Hal didn't say anything. Hal hadn't said much of anything for three days. He was a poor horseman and must be in saddle-blistered agony by now. But his jaw was thick with determination. A good man, Burgade judged: Hal had backbone. Burgade would get Susan back for him. Or die trying. Very likely the latter, he observed without passion.

Burgade's posse left Winslow at a canter, steel-shod hoofs drumming in the starlight, along the right bank of the Little Colorado River towards the Navajo desert. It was just ten or twelve miles west of here that Provo had robbed the Santa Fe train twenty-eight years ago.

CHAPTER SEVEN

'Slow and easy, now,' Provo's voice said in the darkness. 'We won't get another change of horses — these are going to have to do us.' The heavy, raspy voice reached Mike Shelby's ears dimly, as if through a strong crosswind. Everything was a little hazy in Shelby's consciousness; all he wanted in the world was sleep. The horse moved like a rocking chair under him and he had to fight to stay upright on the saddle; several times he almost fell off. At times he thought he'd have preferred to stay in the penitentiary and serve out his time. But he'd only served six months and had another nine and a half years to go. He guessed it would all depend on whether Provo was telling the truth about splitting up his buried cache of railroad gold. In the first place Shelby didn't trust anybody much, and in the second place nobody was a hundred per cent sure Provo even had the gold, let alone was willing to part with it. But one thing was certain: Provo was twice as trail-wise as any of the rest of them. Provo wasn't just bragging when he kept reminding them that without him they'd have been captured a long time ago and sent back to the hole with years added on to their sentences. Provo knew every trick in the book and some that weren't in any book. But Shelby didn't like him much and didn't trust him any more than he trusted anybody else. Shelby hadn't trusted anybody since his mother had run off with a drummer in Nineteen-ought-Five. He'd never known who his father was. His mother had kept company with a lot of men but at least she'd looked after her kid, until the drummer came along. Then she left him behind without even saying good-bye, as if he was an old towel she didn't want to bother to pack.

He was nineteen years old — twenty next month — but he'd covered a lot of ground in his time. He'd been eleven when his mother had left Lordsburg. The fat old Mexican woman who ran the Occidental Café had taken him in, given him bed and board in exchange for the chores Shelby did around the place. About all he could remember about her was standing in the kitchen watching her slap big old corn tortillas from one fat arm to the other. He hadn't stayed long; after his mother pulled out he didn't like Lordsburg much at all. One night he'd stolen a horse and saddle and headed for Silver City. The truant officer picked him up less than five miles out of Lordsburg. They sent him to the county work farm for a year and he met some older and tougher kids there. Shelby was a quick learner. He had a talent for picking the toughest and brightest people around and studying how they did things. He'd hooked up with a fifteen-year-old named Dick Larson and they'd become good friends. When they got out of the work farm they'd hitched over into Texas and terrorised the El Paso area for a winter, living like nomadic savages by stealing chickens and selling stolen horses over in Mexico. When Dick Larson judged it was time, they'd moved on. They'd hung around Brownsville for a while and then drifted back west, on over to Nogales after a couple of years.

Shelby'd been fifteen when he had his first woman, a whore on the Mexican side of Nogales. He and Dick Larson had taken turns with the whore and then robbed her of all her cash and headed back into Arizona.

Dick Larson had an old dime novel, dog-eared and yellowed, about the great train robber Zach Provo, and after reading the whole thing Dick Larson had decided it was easy, the next thing they'd do was rob a train. But the express guard had opened up on them and killed Dick Larson and Shelby had barely got away with his skin.

He'd been lonely after that, almost as much as when his mother had walked out on him. It proved to Shelby that you couldn't depend on anybody for long. He'd lone-wolfed it, strictly, ever since.

He'd done all right until last year when that stupid storekeeper knocked the gun out of his hand and turned him in for armed robbery. Two or three other storekeepers turned up and identified him for several previous crimes, including one he hadn't done, but they convicted him of that one too. He'd gone to Yuma and about the only worthwhile thing about that was meeting Zach Provo.

Shelby had remembered the name from the old dime novel, and meeting Provo in the flesh had been something like meeting royalty. Too much water had gone under the bridge for Shelby to try to team up with Provo the way he had with Dick Larson; anyhow Provo wasn't the type who encouraged hangers-on. But Shelby knew he could learn a lot by watching Provo and studying how Provo worked. He was only nineteen and with luck he had a lot of years ahead of him, but if he was going to survive he had to learn everything there was to learn. Provo was about as good a man to study as any, even if he had been caught and spent twenty-eight years in Yuma. Everybody had bad luck now and then. It didn't mean Provo was anybody's fool.

Dawn came slow. There was a lot of wind-lifted dust in the air and a heavy brownish sky hung over the eastern horizon for half an hour before the sun started to red up. George Weed said, 'What this place needs is a lot more saloons.' His tongue and gums, smiling, were startlingly pink in the black face.

The country was all chopped-up redrock and clay. Shelby didn't know the area at all, but then neither did many other people except the Navajos. The sky seemed a thousand miles wide and the desert just as big. It was high here, several thousand feet of elevation, but the sun came up molten, and by noon Shelby knew it would be far above a hundred degrees on the plain. He felt sullen and cranky and more whacked-out exhausted than he'd ever been in his life.

Provo was up front, leading them. Behind Provo were Taco Riva and Will Gant and Quesada, who was leading the girl's horse. Behind the girl rode Portugee Shiraz. Shelby was next, and Weed was behind him, and a little ways back rode Cesar Menendez. There was no particular reason for everybody to ride single-file now, there was plenty of room to spread out, but they'd got in the habit on the narrow switch-back trails in the Mogollon country behind them.

They came up out of a depression in the ground and Shelby saw a great looming monster of rock four or five miles out ahead. Red-walled, flat-topped, it soared a good thousand feet above the plain. Its shadow ran out a long way along the desert. At the foot of it, hard to see in the shadows, was enough greenery to suggest the presence of water. Provo called back along the line: 'Castle Butte. Little Navajo town down there. We're going in. Everybody act real friendly.'

The Navajo Reservation was bigger than most Eastern states. Here and there, at a crossroads or a good water source, a little community could be found, centred around an Agency trading post and a Navajo Agency police station.

It took them three quarters of an hour to reach Castle Butte. The citizens were up and around: several fat women in elaborate dresses, full of suspicion, watched them ride in. If anybody recognised Zach Provo there was no sign of it. A heavyset Indian in a khaki shirt and cowboy hat low over his eyes came out on to the porch of the trading post and Provo spoke to him in a tongue Shelby had never heard before. The Indian tipped his head back to see out from under his hat and grinned briefly with very bad teeth and rattled off something to which Provo responded with a grunt and a nod. Provo turned and spoke over his shoulder:

'Get on up to the spring there, under the trees. Get cleaned up and eat and try to get some rest. I'll be along in a while. Got some business to transact here. Shelby, you look after missy, she's your responsibility, hear?'

Shelby knew what that meant. He hadn't missed the way Gant and Portugee and Quesada had been watching Susan Burgade. It was a mystery to Shelby why Provo cared one way or the other about the girl's virtue, since Provo wasn't much of a moralist under the best of circumstances and the girl's father was the one man in the world Provo hated more than all the others combined. But presumably there was a reason for it. Shelby didn't want the assignment but he could see why Provo had picked him for it. Probably figured he was too young to have eyes for an older woman — she had to be anyhow ten, twelve year older than Shelby — and besides, Provo trusted him more than most of the others. Shelby didn't know whether to feel flattered or hurt by that, but at the moment he was too tired to care. He didn't want to sit up nursemaiding Miss Burgade, he resented the assignment, and so he was curt and rude to her when he untied her leg from the stirrup-leather and let her climb down stiffly; he stuck close to her while she went over to the spring and splashed water all over her head and face. She was still wearing the homespun dress she'd had on when they'd first seen her — there hadn't been time for anybody to change clothes. This was the first stand-down they'd had since Friday noon, and it was now what, Monday morning? He'd lost track.

Some of them had the knack of sleeping in the saddle. Provo, for one; Provo hadn't looked at all tired when he'd disappeared into the Agency police shack a hundred yards back down the slope from the spring. Riva, of course — Riva had been born on a horse; Riva was fussing over the horses now as if they were expensive Thoroughbreds on a racing paddock and he was their trainer, instead of him being an ex-mountain bandit and them being ordinary old quarter-horse plugs from some working outfit outside Winslow. Riva went around loosening all the cinches and dumping the saddles and blankets, making sure all the horses were within browsing distance of graze tufts, and rubbing them down one at a time with a currybrush he'd stolen somewhere back along the trail.

Not everybody was that solicitous or energetic. George Weed was flat on his back; he started snoring within two minutes after they got dismounted. Portugee Shiraz took the time to find a comfortable bed of leaves under a shade tree fifty yards from the rest of them; Portugee was asleep too. Shelby wished to hell he could do the same, but he wasn't of a mind to disobey Provo's instructions — not yet, at any rate. He wasn't going to follow Provo blindly into the jaws of death but he was willing to suspend resistance until he saw imminent danger. Until then, Shelby judged, he was better off with Provo than without him.

Cesar Menendez sat crosslegged, off a bit from the rest of them, his rifle across his lap, watching with a sleepy-eyed smile, his eyes squinting up so that Shelby couldn't really tell if he was awake or asleep until he saw Menendez stretch like a cat and roll up a cigarette from the makings he'd pinched off that beat-up old wrangler he'd shot in the leg. Menendez dragged on the cigarette and jetted smoke.

Shelby washed some of the grit off his face and told the girl to sit down under a tree and sleep if she could. She made no answer, but she did what he told her to do. She didn't seem to be asleep. Maybe after all she'd been able to sleep on horseback. God knew she'd had nothing better to do. Shelby slid down with his back against a tree and let his legs sprawl out in front of him and concentrated on keeping his dry raw eyes open, mainly because Will Gant was squatting nearby with his face turned towards the girl. Gant was a tense, huge shape in the leaf shadows. He picked up a twig and burrowed it into his ear, examining it and threw it way. He kept staring at the girl; once his eyes glanced towards Shelby and Shelby saw an abrupt touch of sullenness in his face. Then the thick sun-chapped lips pulled back slowly in a smile and Gant sat back with his hands intertwined across the sag of his paunch.

Riva came in and broke out the mess gear and served up some cold food for those who were awake and hungry. The girl ate as if her mind was a thousand miles away on other things. Will Grant dipped his face close to the tin plate and shovelled oversized mouthfuls of food into his face; washed them down with canteen water, only half chewed, his Adam's apple bulging and bouncing in the thick throat.

Riva, who of them all seemed least disturbed by the nerves of flight, sat down loosely and said in a friendly way, 'I feel hound-dog lazy,' and went to sleep smiling.

They had probably been there an hour, but Provo hadn't appeared yet from the police shack. Shelby began to feel spooked. But then, he thought, if the Agency police had arrested Provo they'd be up here by now. He tried to relax.

Presently Portugee woke up and ambled over to squat down beside Will Gant. Portugee's feet were like paddles. The two of them sat there and boasted about the fights they had been in and the carnage they had done, as if there was some important kind of *machismo* in having done and seen such things — or perhaps in being able to talk of it with suitably callous heartiness. Maybe they were trying to impress the girl, but if so, she gave no sign she was listening.

Once, Portugee's glance came around and lay speculatively against Shelby, and something struggled fiercely behind Portugee's eyes. Shelby sat like a stone, not liking this. He pinched his mouth tight and breathed deep through his nose. Will Gant looked at him and Portugee whispered something, and Gant laughed silently, his eyes wrinkling up until they were almost shut. Something was going on between those two. Shelby began to sweat.

Shelby got slowly to his feet and tried to look casual. He wandered over to the spring and had a drink, filled his canteen and wandered back. But he stopped much closer to the girl than he'd been before. He hunkered down on his heels not five feet from her and when she looked at him, her eyes widened: plainly the same thought had crossed her mind that had crossed his.

His manoeuvre had not gone unnoticed. Will Gant stood up and hitched at his trousers with the flats of his wrists. Then he tipped his hat back. The sweatband had indented a red weal across his forehead; he rubbed it with the side of his index finger while he looked unblinkingly at the girl and smiled that slow thick-lipped smile of his.

Damp with springwater, the homespun dress clung to the girl's body, stuck to the undersides of her nubile breasts. She wore no stays, no evident underpinnings of any kind. Her woman-smell reached Shelby's nostrils and he knew the fire that had caught inside Gant and Portugee; it burned him as well. But Shelby couldn't fathom the mind of anybody who would take it from a woman who didn't want to give it. He felt suddenly and unaccountably protective towards her. It had nothing to do with Provo's orders. Sweating, he wiped his palms dry on the buttocks of his Levi's.

From where he squatted he could see past the lovely long column of her back and the dark long hair that she had plaited at the side of her head – past her surly and beautiful face to Gant and Portugee. Portugee removed his hat and slicked back his hair and looked at Will Gant, whereupon Gant got to his feet and shoved his hand down behind his belt buckle into his fly and said, 'Mike, what do you say we climb into that juicy saddle of hers? You can go first, kid, I don't mind watchin'.'

Shelby's lids drooped bleakly. He saw the girl slide her glance off Gant as if he were some kind of zoo animal. With his free hand Gant tugged at the long black hair in his nose. Shelby said, 'Cut it out. You heard Zach.'

'Zach ain't here,' Portugee murmured, and got to his feet. 'You ain't fixin' to spoil the fun are you?'

'Aeah,' Shelby sighed, 'I guess I am, Portugee.' He eased himself upright and planted his boots a couple of feet apart.

Portugee laughed softly. 'Let's bust him, Will.'

The girl was getting up too. Her breasts moved when she turned. She pinched her lower lip with her teeth and gave Shelby a frightened frown.

Gant said, 'Only aimin' to do her a kandness, Mike. She gonna enjoy it, you know she will.'

Shelby drew out his gun and spoke from a semi-crouch: 'Forget it. I like you all right, Will, but we don't need you. I don't want to have to shovel dirt in your fat face.'

Portugee rose up on his dignity. 'Ain't no call for you to pull iron on us, Mike.'

'Just back off, then, and I'll put it away. I've got no fight with you two.'

Portugee and Gant looked at each other. They were wavering, and Shelby helped them along: 'You know damn well both of you together couldn't pour piss out of a hat if the instructions were written on the brim. Fooling with me can only buy you wooden suits — either from me or from Zach when he gets back. Come on now, be sensible. Go on over in the woods and jack your rocks off if you need to, but leave her be.'

Gant took his hand out of his pants. Colour suffused his face. Absurdly he said, 'That ain't no way to talk in front of a lady.'

It made Menendez, over in the shade, laugh until he almost ruptured himself.

Provo came into the trees on his horse. His crag of a face was stern, the dark eyes had a hard glitter. 'Assholes,' he said, voice grating in his windpipe. 'You fools have got a fucking gift for trouble. Leave you alone five minutes and you find some stupid way to bring us grief. I told you two bastards to keep your pants buttoned. And you, Mike, you made a mistake pulling that gun — but once you pulled it you should've used it. Don't pull iron on a man unless you're fixing to shoot him.'

Portugee said uncomfortably, 'Shit, you don't miss much, do you?'

Shelby, stiff and stung by the rebuke, said defensively, 'I'd have used it if they'd forced it. Hell, I didn't need to.'

'Then you shouldn't have pulled it.'

'Jesus, Zach, even Menendez thought it was all a big laugh.'

'Balls. We can't afford a killing here, the Navajos won't put up with it. Menendez was right to head it off. He used his head. Maybe you'll learn to use yours if you live long enough. Now everybody gather round here.'

The others drifted in. Shelby went to take Susan Burgade's elbow but she jerked galvanically when he touched her. He stayed with her and listened to Provo from where he stood.

'We're all set. They'll side with us as long as we treat them friendly. Everybody remember that. Anybody lays one finger on a Navajo and I'll personally cut that finger off.'

Will Gant said, 'How'd you do it, Zach?'

'Reminded them it's white men after us and white men's money we stole. I told them it's Burgade back there. Everybody up here knows it was Burgade killed my wife. She was a fullblood Navajo and she was innocent as the day she was born; she didn't have a thing to do with Burgade's fight with me and the people know it. So Sam Burgade ain't about to get any favours from these people.

'That posse's bound to pull in here soon,' he continued. 'The Navajo police will keep them busy a few hours and then they'll turn the posse back to the Reservation line — white man's law can't set foot on this Reservation. Burgade figures to come on after us, and he's good enough to slip through past the Agency police unless he's got awful dumb or awful unlucky in his old age, but he's just one man. I am to set him up where I want him and kill the old bastard one bullet at a time.'

Susan's eyes were almost closed. She swayed on her feet. Shelby reached out to prop her up but she shoved herself away from him. Her rigid back expressed rage and terror all at once. Shelby felt vaguely uncomfortable. He didn't care what happened to Sam Burgade — everybody's father had to die sometime. But it made him uneasy to see what it was doing to Susan. Listening to Provo talk about his dead wife made him pretty sure Provo had something just as ugly in mind for Burgade's daughter.

Will Gant, who was shrewder than he looked, said, 'Hepping us can get these Innuns in trouble with the Innun Bureau. You must of done a heap of persuading.'

Offhandedly Provo said, 'Sure. But I told them where they could go dig up ten thousand dollars in gold to help folks out on the Reservation. Up here ten thousand dollars is more than the whole tribe sees in a year. They'll side with us long enough to suit me. By the time the Bureau starts leaning on them we'll be long gone.'

'Ten thousand,' Shelby said. 'You said you had forty-eight thousand buried.'

'You don't think I was stupid enough to cache it all in one place, do you? It's scattered in four hideouts. One cache, maybe somebody could stumble across it by accident. But not four of them.'

'Smart,' Shelby said, and filed it: one more good lesson to memorise.

Will Gant was looking at Susan with a strange light in his eyes. 'What we aiming to do about her, Zach?'

Provo smiled a little, not with his eyes. He quoted softly, 'Patient, ever patient, and joy shall be thy share. Bear that in mind and you'll be all right. Will. Just don't crowd things.' He looked at the girl and his gentle laughter had the cruel dry sound of dead leaves rattling in an autumn wind.

Don't get too het up about her problems, Shelby told himself. *You got enough of your own.*

Provo said, 'Taco, Quesada, saddle 'em up.'

The two of them turned and went. George Weed went with them.

Portugee said, 'Where we going now?'

'Down the Little Colorado,' Provo said. 'Redrock country. I've got a place in mind up between Cedar Ridge and Marble Canyon.'

'That where you got the rest of that gold hid?'

'That'd be telling,' Provo said. He smiled with his mouth again. 'But I ain't got a double-cross in mind. I saw you thinking about what happened to Lee Roy, but Lee Roy was no good, you could see that. He'd have found some way to get us all killed. You'll get your share of the gold, Portugee.'

'That's right,' Portugee said. 'I will. But what then?'

'Then you can go wherever you want. Personally I'd recommend northeast. Nobody's going to track up through the Rockies. Straight on up through Colorado and Wyoming and Montana. Right into Canada and maybe ship out from Vancouver. But that's up to you-all.'

'What about you?' Shelby said.

'Me?' Provo laughed unpleasantly. 'All I want is Sam Burgade.'

CHAPTER EIGHT

The Navajo policemen subjected the posse to the long-winded rigmarole of formal protocol. After an hour of argument during which nobody budged and everybody remained excessively polite, Sam Burgade uttered a curse and stamped outside the Agency police shack. A blowsy woman gave him a flat stare of evident dislike and made a point of absenting herself from his vicinity. A stray vesper brought to his nostrils a malodorous outhouse smell.

Nye came outside and said, 'We ain't about to change their mands, Captain.'

'I know. Provo got to them.'

'What you reckon he give them?'

'A lot of sweet talk and some of that Santa Fe gold he's got buried up here.'

'I'd admire to bust rat through here and keep after them, but I don't reckon that'd set well with the federal gov'ment. They don't cotton to anybody pushin' on to the Reservation without the Navajos allow it. All them bleedin' hawts back East git all up in arms about white folks bustin' treaties. My deppities and me could maybe get in dutch, but rat now I don't reckon that's my main worry. Main thing is, Captain, I'm a sworn officer of the law. If I go on after Provo now I'm bustin' the law. I'm out of my bailiwick on Navajo land, I got no authority here at all.'

'I know that, Noel.'

'Gravels hell out of me to let you down, Captain.'

'You've got your duty.'

'Yes, sir, I do. But I sure don't lak it much.' Nye's eyes flickered when they touched his. 'Captain, we got to turn back.'

'I won't argue with you.'

'You got to come back with us.'

Burgade's silence argued with him.

'Captain, you got no authority here neither. You got no right on Innun land.'

'I guess that's between me and the Indians, isn't it,' Burgade said. 'I'll take my chances.'

'You ain't got no chance, Captain.' Nye's voice had gone harsh, angry more with himself than with Burgade. 'They's seven men out there alongside of Provo. Eight men you got to fight alone. You cain't do that, no way. And don't you know it's exactly what Provo wants you to do?'

'Yes, I know that.'

'Then quit pretending lak you just too damn proud to quit. You ain't a stupid man.'

A knotted muscle rippled in Burgade's cheek. 'Provo needs me the way the axe needs the turkey. If I don't keep after him he'll have no more use for Susan — he'll set his dogs on her.'

'You better stop and study on that awhile. You fixing to make a powerful mistake. Those eight convicts put you under a gun, I don't know but one way it can come out. You got to die. You dying ain't going to hep Susan none.'

'Everybody's got to die,' Burgade breathed, 'but nobody's got to give up.'

'Shit, Captain, that's a fine sentiment but it don't cut no ice with me. You got sixteen million acres of Navajo Reservation out yonder. No shade except maybe your own shadow. You fixing to go out into that and bust your lance against them eight men awmed to the teeth. And up against all that, the only thang you got left is knowing you ain't going to give up? Shit. Zach Provo'll trample you under and never even look back to see what-all he stepped on.'

Burgade's toes curled inside his boots. His face was a bitter mask.

Nye looked straight ahead, not at him. 'Captain, if I got to say it all, I will. You don't even ride good no more. You just too cocksucking old to fight.'

In the blinding sunshine every shadow was black and had

a sharp edge. The heat sucked sweat from Burgade's pores. Hal Brickman came out of the police shack and stood under the porch shade within earshot.

Burgade said, 'I haven't got a lot of time to argue with you, Noel. But maybe you'll understand this. If I turn back now, knowing what they'll do to Susan, I don't think I'd last a week without putting a gun in my mouth and pulling the trigger.'

'I know how you feel about that, Captain, but you forgetting one of two thangs. It ain't going to take but five, six days, maybe a week, before we get enough pressure against the Navajo Council from Washington on down to allow us to bring posses on to the Reservation.'

'By that time Susan will be dead and the gang will be a thousand miles from here. Hell, Noel, getting off this Reservation's no harder than getting on to it. There's no fence. They're free to sneak out of here anywhere along a thousand miles of boundary and we won't have any idea where to look.'

'Could be. But forget Zach Provo, Captain. I'm only thanking about your daughter. Look, Provo don't want to kill Susan, he's only using her for bait. Shit, if he kills her he's obliged to get every awmed man in the United States after his hide. He knows what's got to happen to him if he kills her. Even them Agency police will be on his ass. He won't have no place left to hide out. He cain't afford that. No, Captain. He fands out you ain't on his track, and he'll turn Susan loose. It's the only thang he can do.'

Hal Brickman stepped out of the shade and came forward. 'Maybe the sheriff's right about that, you know. Provo's smart enough to know what'll happen to him if Susan comes to any harm.

'If you knew Provo better you wouldn't think that way.'

Nye said, 'Provo's a lot of things but he ain't stupid.'

'If he cared about his own skin,' Burgade said, 'he wouldn't have kidnapped Susan in the first place. He had plenty of chances to get clean away, out of the country. He didn't. He came after me instead. Listen — he's lived the past twenty-eight years for one thing. Revenge. He doesn't care whether he lives or dies, so long as he takes me with him and makes me suffer along the way. If I turn back now, he'll only have one way left to make me suffer.'

Hal Brickman's eyes widened. 'You mean kill Susan.'

'That's it. If I don't show up where Provo can see me in the next twenty-four hours, she'll be dead, and he'll see to it I find out about it.'

Nye's voice began to climb unreasonably. 'But god-damnit, Captain. S'posin' you do show up? S'posin' you take his bait? What good'll that do Susan?'

'Maybe he'll make a trade,' Burgade murmured.

Nye stared at him. 'You for Susan, you mean.'

'He might do it.'

'Jesus goddamn Christ.'

The deputies came out of the shack, followed by two uniformed Navajo police who stood on the porch and folded their arms and watched while the posse got mounted. Burgade said, 'I'll have to ride back with you until we're out of sight.'

Little grey birds flitted soundlessly from the roof of the police shack to the treetops up by the spring. Burgade locked both hands around the saddle horn and hauled himself up by an effort of will. Riding away from the village, Nye said to him, 'Jesus, Captain, you ain't in no fit shape.'

'Shut up.'

They batted south along the tawny earth, everybody in a bitter frame of mind. It took forty-five minutes to get beyond the line of sight of the Castle Butte village. Nye said, 'Maybe you ought to ride back at least as far as the line. You know damn well they gonna come out here in a little while to see if we kep our word.'

'I can't waste that much time, Noel.'

The posse came to a ragged halt. Nye's unrevealing eyes swept bleakly across them. 'Moorhead, you mand swappin' horses with the Captain? I believe you got the best horse of the bunch there.'

'I'll keep this one.' Burgade didn't want to have to dismount and climb up again. He said, 'But I'd take it kindly if some of you'd let me have a little spare food and a couple of canteens.'

'You heard the Captain. Pony up, boys.'

Hal Brickman kneed his horse forward. 'I could use some provisions too, Sheriff.'

Burgade said, 'Forget it, Hal.'

'No. I'm going with you.'

'I appreciate the gesture, Hal, but — '

'If I turn back now and anything happens to Susan, I'll feel exactly the same way you'd feel. You've got to see that.'

A gust of wind came along, like a breath from an oven. The hovering glare had given Burgade a headache. He studied Hal over a long stretch of time and finally he said, 'You stand an excellent chance of being killed if you ride with me. You accept that?'

'Yes, sir. I know I'm a greenhorn but I can shoot. I'll do what you tell me to do.'

Nye said, 'God knows you could use the hep, Captain.'

'All right, Hal. It's your decision.'

'Thank you, sir.'

'Don't thank me, for God's sake.'

They looked back a couple of times and saw the posse's dust receding to the south. Burgade chose a westerly course that kept them below the horizon, running along dry watercourses and the groined notches between low hills. 'We'll circle around and try to pick up their tracks north of Castle Butte.' The strong sun slashed at them, hot breezes raked them with sinister abrasive caresses, there wasn't a vestige of shade anywhere; sweat was sticky in the small of his back, in his palms, in his crotch, on his lips and throat. He had got inured to the smell of himself.

An eagle passed high overhead with a steady wing-beat. The empty land was a match for Burgade's emptiness of spirit. Sixteen million acres, Nye had said, and that was just about exactly the size of it. The Reservation sprawled all over the high desert, overlapping the boundaries of four states. Most of it was just like this – a leafless sun-blasted furnace, broken here and there by craggy mesas and cutbank arroyos and the deep-canyon tributaries of the Colorado: the Grand Canyon was just a little way to the northwest.

It was a hard-mouthed horse, a small tough grey gelding. Burgade set a pace to conserve the animals — walk, trot, canter, then walk again. The grey fought the bit at every turning.

Hal didn't speak unless spoken to. It was a silent ride for the first hour, and then, partly to keep himself awake, Burgade began to talk. 'Can you use that gun?'

'I said I could, sir.'

'I know what you said.'

'I'm a good target-shooter. I've never shot at a man.'

'Think it over, then. If the toughs see you with a gun in your hand they'll assume you know how to handle it. It'll only encourage them to use theirs first.'

'Yes, sir. But I don't imagine they'll need much encouraging from me.'

'Yes, I expect that's so,' Burgade said. 'Look, they're on the run from the hangman. They killed two prison guards and left a man dead at the smelter. That makes them all equally guilty of first-degree murder in the eyes of the law. Now, even leaving Susan aside, you know what that means.'

'Yes, sir. I have a pretty good idea what they'll do to anybody who gets in their way.'

'Keep your head down, then, and don't smile at any strange faces. These men are quick and they're short-fused.'

About four in the afternoon they found tracks. Burgade didn't dismount for a close-up look. Hal said, 'How do we know these are the right tracks?'

'Not likely to be more than one party this big out here today.'

'Maybe they're older — maybe they're from a week ago. How can you tell?'

'By the amount of dust the wind's blown into the prints. These are only a few hours old. Look there at the horse droppings.'

There was a line of muffin-droppings, undoubtedly still soft and warm: they were still green.

The tracks went straight into the northwest. They kept moving into the waning afternoon. To keep from falling asleep Burgade told Hal everything he could remember about Provo and those of Provo's men he had known. Hal seemed to take it all in — Portugee Shiraz's fondness for knives, George Weed's extraordinary skill with guns, Provo's weakness for unnecessary complexities in trying to outguess his opponents. It was the bewildering intricacy of Provo's scheme that had tripped him up twenty-eight years ago. 'He'd have got away clean if he hadn't tried to be quite so tricky. He may be making the same mistake this time.'

'What was his mistake?'

'He didn't run for it when he should have. He decided to bluff it out.'

'I never did hear about that. How it really happened, I mean.'

The Santa Fe trains used to stop for water west of Winslow on the way up the Flagstaff grade. Provo planted a whacking big charge of blasting powder along the ties where he knew the express car would stand. He didn't know much about explosives but he didn't take any chances. Blew up the whole car — disintegrated it sky-high. There were several guards inside, it blew them all to pieces. Provo picked up the gold while the smoke was still settling and inside of three or four minutes he was headed out on his horse. He had a bandanna mask and he didn't figure on anybody recognising him. He shouldn't have taken that chance. If he'd been a little smarter he'd have sent his wife away before he robbed the train, and he'd have met her in Mexico later on. We'd never have found him.'

'But you did. How?'

'Three or four people on the train recognised him.'

'Even with a mask on?'

'Two of them were Indians. They'd known him for years. He's got a hunched way of moving, very quick, tense. And they recognised his horse and his clothes. There wasn't any mistake about the identification.'

'But how'd you catch him?'

'He walked into it. He spent five or six days back in the redrock country — up where he appears to be headed now. He buried the gold somewhere back there and then he went right back home to his hogan down near Salina Springs. We were waiting for him.'

'Wasn't his wife killed?'

The sun had dried the spit in Burgade's mouth. It was a moment before he answered. His words had a dry rustle. 'She was.'

'I understand he blames you for that.'

'It was my bullet that killed her.'

Hal didn't say anything. He looked sorry he'd asked the question. They went down the steep bank of an arroyo, leaning far back in their saddles.

Burgade said, 'Provo was being clever. When we showed ourselves he tried to bluff it out. Denied the whole thing. It was no good, it tripped him up. When he saw we weren't buying it, he elected to try to shoot his way out. I returned his fire. His wife was behind him, inside the hogan where none of us could see her. My bullet went through Provo's thigh — I was shooting to knock him down, not kill him. Went right through him and struck his wife in the throat. She was a damned handsome Navajo girl, expecting a baby. I have regretted it every day for the past twenty-eight years.'

'If he made a break for it with a gun, he had to expect the consequences. I don't see how you can go on blaming yourself forever, sir.'

'I don't blame myself. I just regret it happened. It was an accident, which Provo doesn't choose to accept.'

'An accident he brought on himself. And on her.'

'Just so,' Burgade said stonily. 'But you understand it

hasn't been an easy memory to live with, regardless of who was to blame.'

The sun threw a last burst of light along the cloudy horizon. He saw one pale star. They kept running northwesterly, following the tracks through a country which was starting to buckle and heave. Into the breaks of the canyon country. In the next hour the darkness condensed and a heavier mass of cloud moved in. By eight o'clock the night was viscous as syrup. Burgade halted the grey and said reluctantly, 'Can't track till those clouds blow over. Let's step down and eat.'

'Yes, sir. We could both use some sleep.'

'We'll see. We don't want to give them too much of a lead. But it's just as dark where they are as it is here, and the country's rougher up that way. They've probably been forced to stop too. Anyhow we can get a little rest until the clouds move on.'

'You don't think it's going to rain, do you? That would wash out their tracks.'

'It won't rain tonight,' Burgade said, with only a glance at the clouds.

They loosened the cinches and hobbled the horses. Hal broke out provisions and they ate a cold meal; there was no risking a fire. Pemmican and hardrock biscuits, tinned peaches and canteen water — that was their supper. Afterwards Burgade mumbled, 'No point trying to stand guard. They won't double back yet. Get some sleep. I'll wake you.' Without waiting to see if Hal obeyed, he lay back on the ground with his hat for a pillow and stared at the underbellies of the clouds. He was in a disoriented haze; he had spent so many days fighting to keep awake he was sure he was too tired to sleep. The waking nightmare of reality rubbed inside his brain like coarse grit, driving him towards madness. He saw little likelihood he would ever emerge from it; he had put out of his mind the possibility of surviving this. To get Susan out alive would be miracle enough.

Staring at the black sky, he carefully opened small gates to let Susan's haunting image flow into his mind. In a while her face hovered before him and he could hear her singing the way she did sometimes in the kitchen, in her small true voice.

He wondered if Hal's thoughts were like his own. Hal was a good boy. Boy, he thought, Hal was thirty-three or thirty-four, a successful mining engineer — no boy. He handled himself well and had not complained of the endless hours of rough riding. If Hal had a basic weakness, Burgade thought, it was not cowardice or squeamishness. But Hal tended to be too impetuous. He had been an athlete in his school years; he was handsome and self-confident and a lot of things had come easily to him. There was a chance his very abilities would be his downfall. His athletic co-ordination was great, like his stamina — but if he'd been a little less agile, a little more accident-prone, he'd have taken his knocks by now, learned his lesson, learned how to be more cautious.

Burgade's mind drifted. His exhaustion was physical, emotional, mental, all compounded by tense strain carried to the taut limits of tolerance. Sleep moved towards him, silent and black.

He awoke fuzzily. He was lying on his side. He did not stir; he kept his eyes shut and his breathing deep and even. Someone was behind him.

He heard a foot crunch gravel and the tentative clearing of a throat, and he made a face and rolled over. 'Next time you come up behind a man,' he said, 'announce yourself. I almost blew your head off.'

Hal said, 'I was deciding whether to wake you up. The clouds have cleared off.'

'Time's it?'

'About two, by my watch.'

Burgade looked around. Dust around the horned moon was a luminous ring. The light was enough to see by. 'I slept six hours,' he said. 'Too long. They've got another hour or two on us now.'

'From what you say,' Hal observed, 'I expect they'll wait

for us to catch up when they get to wherever it is they're going.'

Burgade grunted. He looked past Hal and saw the two horses standing thirty or forty feet away, saddled and ready. Hal had packed everything up. It annoyed Burgade slightly people were always doing things for him, this trip. But what irritated him far more was the fact that the noise hadn't awakened him. *I can't sleep again until we've finished this business,* he decided.

The sleep hadn't revived him. He felt logy and weak. He stumbled once on his way to the horse. But Hal was considerate enough not to try to help him climb into the saddle.

He found the tracks without much trouble and lifted the grey to a trot. Hal rode alongside in brooding silence for ten or fifteen minutes before he revealed what was eating him. 'Sir, I had better know what you've got in mind to do.'

'Do?'

'You told the sheriff you were going to try to trade your life for Susan's.'

'So I did.'

'Is that still your plan?'

'It never has been. I lied to Noel — to get him off my back.'

Hal's face was turned towards him. Under the hatbrim his expression was invisible. But his voice was slightly choked. 'You mean you never intended to offer a trade?'

'You're thinking if there was a chance in a thousand you could save Susan's life by offering your own in exchange, you'd do it like that.' He snapped his fingers.

'You're damn right I would.'

'That's very fine and noble,' Burgade said, stiffly.

'Let me tell you something. Zack Provo's not going to strike any bargains. Why should he, when he's got a corner on the market?'

'It appears to me, sir, that we're still obliged to try.'

'Put it this way, Hal. Two enemies face each other with knives. They crouch and circle each other, looking for an opening. One of them is an expert knife-thrower, the other one isn't. Suppose you're the expert knife-thrower. What do you do? Throw your knife?'

It puzzled Hal. 'I don't know.'

'No. You don't throw. Because you're enemy's in a crouch and you can't be sure of finishing him with one toss. And once you've thrown your knife you're defenceless. So you keep your knife and you fight your enemy on his terms.'

'I'm not sure I follow that, sir.'

'My freedom of action is the only weapon I've got. If I turned myself in to Provo as part of some sort of trade, I'd be giving up my only threat against him. You see, he's not going to kill Susan as long as I'm out here with guns.'

'Then what's he going to do?'

'He's going to try to take me alive,' Burgade said in a tired voice. 'He'll want to force me to watch them do . . . things . . . to Susan. He wants me to watch her die. And then he'll find a slow way to kill me. He'll take his time because it's going to dawn on him that killing me will leave a great big hole where his hate used to be. He's going to miss me — he won't like the idea of ending all the years of hating my guts.'

The tracks curled behind the knee of a steep hill which threw a shadow across them. Burgade had to slow the grey to a walk and lean down to see the ground. The steel horseshoes had left shallow indentations in the hard ground. Twenty miles ahead loomed a mountain range, a dark heavier mass against the broken clouds and stars.

Hal said, 'But what can we do, then?'

'Try to get at Provo. Pick him off. The rest of them will probably be willing to let Susan go in return for their own chance to get away.'

'That's a long shot, isn't it?'

'It's the only shot we've got.'

'But how can we get close enough to Provo to capture him?'

'I said nothing about capture.'

He heard the quick hiss of Hal's indrawn breath. 'You

mean kill him. Shoot him from ambush. Is that it? I'm not sure I could do that, sir.'

'Nobody's asked you to.'

Hal, not knowing what to say, curbed his tongue. They came out of the hill shadow and followed the prints along the flat towards the distant mountains. Inside Burgade, a hard knot grew, a pain of ugly lust that demanded violence — deeper, stronger than the will to live.

The plain wrinkled up towards the mountains' jagged upheaval. By mid-morning Burgade was in the foothills. The sun was a merciless, molten orange; the dazzling brilliance made his eyes swim. The hills made hard going for the horses: there were acres of looming boulders that weighed hundreds, even thousands, of tons.

Hal said, 'Where are we?'

'Close to the west boundary. These mountains run about thirty miles thick. Beyond that you get into the deep gorge country — Grand Canyon. They wouldn't be that far west — they'd be cut off with their backs to the gorges. Provo wouldn't lock his back door that way. They'll stay in these mountains.'

They climbed steadily at a slow gait. Red cliffs leaned back high above them like exploded wreckage on a deserted battlefield. There were great swaths of pine timber standing in lancers' order. The meadows and clearings were yellow with shortgrass. Hal said, 'These tracks seem to be headed back downhill.'

'No. A man bends the grass down in the direction he's walking. A horse does the opposite.'

'Do you suppose they're where they can see us from up there?'

'If they're not, they will be. Stay inside the trees as much as you can and don't skyline yourself.'

Black-bellied clouds assembled over the westward peaks during the afternoon. By six o'clock the two horsemen were high in pine country, plodding their tired animals uphill along needle-blanketed slopes. The fugitive's tracks went into a sun-splattered stream but did not come out on the opposite bank.

Hal said, 'They've gone in the water to hide their tracks.'

Burgade grunted. He eased himself out of the saddle and had a long look around, turning slowly on the balls of his feet. Finally he took one of the canteens off his saddle — the empty one — and dipped it into the stream. It bubbled and filled. He set it down on the ground long enough for the mud and debris to settle to the bottom before he drank from it. The horses were guzzling from the stream.

'You may as well step down. We'll wait here a bit.'

'What for?'

'Sundown. They kept going west up this stream, and I'm not about to follow along after them this time of day. Not with that sun in my eyes.'

'But they'll gain two hours on us.'

'They're not going far now,' Burgade said. 'Beyond that pass to west of here, there's a steep drop towards the gorge country. Provo's somewhere right around here. I'd guess not more than three miles from us right now. At sunset we'll scout around — on foot. Plenty of time. Why don't you break us out something to eat? A man can't fight on an empty belly.'

Hal gave him a bleak look of dulled anger. Probably couldn't understand how he could act so casual and callous. Burgade lay down in a thicket of brush and kept turning his head slowly from side to side so as not to miss any stray sound. A lot of things were flooding back into his conscious memory and he didn't want to interrupt the flow. It had been thirty years since he'd ridden scout for General Crook but he needed to remember everything now, every nuance. His only chance was to be a better Indian than Zach Provo.

He sat up to eat, and went to the stream to wash the camp pans and scrub his face. The sun was lodged in pinetops upstream and it was a good time for an ambush from that direction, and so he took Hal and the horses and faded back into the timber along the east face of a hill which blocked the sun from view. They waited there for almost an hour. Then walked back to the stream, leading the horse. The twilight was cool and breezy; pine branches rustled overhead and the stream gurgled. Burgade walked along the bank, upstream, until he saw enough pale dots in the water to be sure. 'They went up this way.'

'How can you tell?'

'Horses kicked over a lot of pebbles. Look.' He reached down into the water, up to his elbow, and picked up a small stone. 'Rough side up. It's been turned over recently — otherwise it would have been smooth and slimy like the other side.'

They walked very slowly up the bank. After ten minutes Burgade was trying to conceal the fact that he was breathing hard. He stopped and scowled at the heavy carpet of black clouds that was unrolling swiftly overhead. 'We'll have rain tonight.'

'Does that mean we might lose them?'

'Provo will make sure we don't.' Burgade had been weighing things in his mind. Now he said with abrupt decision, 'He's not going to leave anything to chance. He's got to be right around here someplace — three miles, maybe five, but no more than that. Otherwise he wouldn't have bothered to ride in the water.'

'And?'

'He knows we're close to him. He's probably doubled back on his own tracks and set up an ambush. I don't see any point in walking into it.'

'Then what do we do?'

'Nothing. We camp and sit tight. When we don't show up, he'll send somebody out to look for us.'

'What if he does?'

'We'll just wait for whoever it is to show up.' The trees crowded down close along both banks of the stream. The dusk was thickening, made darker by swelling storm clouds. Burgade spent ten minutes walking around in the trees until he found a spot that satisfied him. 'We'll picket the horses in here and roll up a couple of fake blanket dummies to look like men asleep. Doubtful anybody'll fall for it, but whoever comes will investigate. We'll set a little snare for him.'

'With what?'

Burgade rummaged in his saddlebags. 'This.' He took out the coil of fine high-test fishing line.

The rain held off. Burgade showed Hal how to string the line, at shin level, taut from tree to tree. There wasn't enough to go all the way around but it wasn't likely an intruder would expose himself by stepping across the stream, so Burgade left that side open. The rest was circled by the tripwire.

By the time they were finished it was full dark. Burgade picked his spot and pushed down on Hal's shoulder. 'Don't even breathe. We don't want him to spot us.'

'What makes you think anyone will come?'

'We didn't cross over the top. Provo had to be watching for us. When we didn't show up, he must have started to worry. He may even think we got lost. He'll send a stalking horse.'

'A what?'

'A man to show himself. Somebody we'll recognise and follow. Meant to lead us into a trap. Now shut up and lie still.'

Burgade sat on the ground with his .30-06 rifle across his lap. Forty feet away, inside the tripwire circle, the picketed horses browsed. He couldn't really see them; the darkness was complete. He spent a quarter of an hour gathering up dry pine needles and lashing them to the end of a two-foot twig in a torch-sized bundle. When that was done he unwrapped his waterproof match bag and put three wooden matches where he could get at them — one behind each ear and one between his teeth in the corner of his mouth like a toothpick. He set the rifle silently aside and palmed his .45 double-action, and then there was nothing more to do but wait, and nothing to think about but Susan.

The shadows were deep and sinister, the darkness all but

total. It was possible to make out the darker outlines of the trees overhead against the clouds beyond, and he could distinguish the boles of nearby trees and the shape of the forest ground, but the horses were only vague suggestions and he had to rely mainly on his ears.

It was hard to think about the anguish Susan must be going through; it was impossible not to think about it. Whether or not they had laid so much as a finger on her, she was living at every breath with the horror of it, the awful knowledge of what Provo aimed to do. Even if she could be rescued alive, would she ever be whole again?

Zach Provo had that to answer for. Burgade knew the rage that burned in Provo. It was no more savage than his own.

He heard the intruder long before he saw anything. The man was trying to be silent but he couldn't help giving himself away. The wind had died, the creek was beyond earshot, there were no sounds at all to muffle the intruder's movements. Whoever it was, it wasn't Provo. Most likely it wasn't Menendez or Taco Riva, either. Those three — and possibly — Quesada — would know better than to move as fast as this one was moving. The sound was off to the right, perhaps a hundred feet away and coming forward on the far side of the horses.

The intruder halted for a while and almost went around behind the wire ring. Probably scouting in a crisscross pattern — but Burgade didn't want him to circle away. He began to sweat in the cool darkness. The revolver stirred in his fist.

Hal stiffened. Burgade touched his shoulder to keep him quiet. Then he had a piece of luck. One of the horses stamped its hoof to get rid of an insect.

The soft thud echoed through the forest. The intruder, wherever he was, froze for several minutes. There wasn't a sound. Burgade could imagine him, turning his face slowly to try to pick up tiny sounds on the flats of his eardrums; keening the night, staring into the darkness as if to burn it away with his gaze.

It was a long time before the intruder moved. Then the faint sounds of his travel crossed from right to left. The man was coming in towards the horses. Burgade lifted the revolver higher in his fist and settled his elbow against his knee.

He still couldn't see the man. He heard him move in from that northerly quadrant, moving a few yards at a time and stopping to listen again. A stray breeze roughed up the pine needles briefly; it must have carried man-smell to the horses, for one of them whickered tentatively, a very quiet throaty sound in the night. The intruder recognised the sound and kept moving forward. He couldn't be more than a few yards from the tripwire, but Burgade couldn't see a thing over there. Several trees were in the way. The tripwire itself was in his line of sight, but he didn't know whether he was going to be able to see the man that far away even if he did step into the view-line: it was fifty feet away and the darkness was intense.

He could hear the taut dry constrictions of Hal's breathing. The intruder seemed to have halted behind the trees just outside the tripwire. Within fifteen or twenty feet of the horses. The man must be able to see the blanket-wrapped dummies from there, the saddles and gear lying about. He would suspect the dummies for what they were. But his mission was to alert Burgade, not to evade him. The man had to move.

But he didn't. A drop of sweat formed on Burgade's forehead, ran down his nose, and dripped on to the back of his left hand. Had the intruder spotted the tripwire? Burgade's grip on the ·45 tightened. He suppressed the sudden urgent need to reach around and scratch the small of his back.

Then the intruder moved, crossing fast from pine to pine — Burgade saw his outline quite plainly, and then, between the trees, the tripwire caught the man just above the ankles and spilled him.

The man fell towards the ground with quite a bit of noise, grabbing at branches to stop his fall. Burgade ran forward five paces, the noise of his own movement covered by the intruder's tumble, and stopped with a clear view of the man.

'I've got a gun aimed at you, friend. Don't move a whisker.'

The intruder hesitated, both elbows on the ground; but it was all right. He'd made his decision when he hadn't started shooting at Burgade's first word.

Burgade moved slowly forward, holding the revolver balanced on the man. 'Come on, Hal.'

The intruder was an amorphous shape in the poor light. But any movement would draw Burgade's fire, and the man seemed to realise that. He didn't stir.

Burgade stopped six feet from him. He handed the torch to Hal and got the matchstick out of his mouth. 'Stay behind me. Light that and let's have a look at him.'

The match exploded into light. By that illumination Burgade took one step forward and kicked the rifle away from the intruder's black fist. He reached down and plucked the the revolver from the holster. Hal had the torch lighted now. The intruder showed his alarm: wild white rings showed around the pupils of his eyes.

'George Weed,' Burgade said. 'Stand up and walk over by the blankets.'

Weed got to his feet, surly and sullen. He didn't talk. He went into the clearing. The butt stock of Hal's rifle protruded from its saddle boot and Burgade saw Weed eyeing it. 'Go ahead. Pick it up and try for me.'

Weed shook his head. 'You've unloaded it.'

'Sure.'

'So you wouldn't of shot me. You was bluffing. You wouldn't of done it.'

'But *you* would have.'

'You bastard, Burgade. You motherfuckin' bastard.' Weed turned around and pulled the crotch of his Levi's down and said, 'All right, hell, you got me, now what you going to do with me?'

'Tie you up,' Burgade said. 'Hold my gun on him, Hal. If he tries anything, shoot him.'

'Yes, sir.' Hal's voice was without tone. Burgade sat Weed down on the ground and tied his hands together behind his back with a rawhide piggin' string. He tied the ankles together and used Weed's own belt to hook the ankles and wrists together so that Weed couldn't straighten out. Burgade kept one eye closed during the entire business and when he had tested the knots and found them secure, he stood up, still with his eye shut, and held his hand out to the side, and spoke to Hal behind him: 'Now hand me back my gun and go douse that torch in the stream.'

The torch moved away from his back, throwing his bobbing shadow longer along the ground and then fading back among the trees. When he heard it sizzle in the water, he opened the eye he had kept closed. It had not been blinded by the light and now, with the one eye, he could see Weed well enough. He slid the revolver into leather and walked back across the tripwire to the spot where he had waited in ambush; picked up his rifle and brought it back into camp. Hal had come back from the creek, still carrying the soaked torch for some reason — Burgade said drily, 'You can throw that away now.'

Weed said, 'What you expect to get out of this, anyway?'

'You were supposed to be a stalking horse, George. You were supposed to let me spot you and then you were supposed to lead me back into Provo's ambush. Fine. Now you're going to tell me where that is.'

'Stick it up your ass, Burgade. You don't get nothing out of me. Nothing, motherfucker, nothing.'

Burgade ran his hands quickly over the man's pockets. Nothing in them but odds and ends. But in Weed's boot top he found a sheath knife. He slipped it out and tested its blade with his thumb. It was a squat heavy knife, made for animal-skinning, not for fighting. It had gone rusty and a little dull. He locked its handle in his fist to weight the knuckles and suddenly clouted Weed across the side of the face.

Weed's head rocked back against the ground. Burgade heard Hal gasp.

A few tiny raindrops came down through the trees. Burgade felt one strike the back of his hand. His knuckles began to hurt. 'I can beat on you for a while, George, until my hands get tired. And then I can start cutting you up with this rusty knife of yours. I don't mind if you bleed to death.'

He heard Hal's taut breathing, full of disapproval, but he didn't look around. He only said, in the same calm voice, 'Now, you know Provo doesn't give a damn about you, George. He picked you to come out here because he figured you were the most expendable of all of them. When you don't come back he'll know I've got you. But it won't worry him. He won't do anything about it. You don't owe him anything, George. And you may as well forget about that buried gold of his, because you've got no chance to get at it now. Either I slice you up and leave you here to bleed to death, or you tell me what I want to know, and I'll leave you tied up until I've done my business here and then we'll take you back to the law. That's your choice.'

'Choice between you killing me and the law hanging me? Hell, Burgade, you got to do better'n that.'

'Maybe if you tell me what I want to know, Provo'll kill me. Then all you've got to worry about is getting yourself untied. You might get away clear.'

Weed showed a double row of white teeth. 'Now, there's a thought, ain't it?'

'Where are they, George? Where's my girl?'

Weed told him.

CHAPTER NINE

SHELBY came awake irritably. Somebody was kicking him in the butt.

'Come on, get up. Your turn to stand guard.' It was Joaquim Quesada. Shelby rolled over and saw it hadn't been a kick after all. Quesada had been hitting him with the stock of his rifle.

'Jesus,' Shelby complained. 'The hell time is it?'

'Quién sabe?' Quesada lay down and wrapped a blanket around him.

Shelby picked up his ·30-30 and walked off a little piece, and sat down in the grass. It was a surly night, the sky was black and wild. Dim suggestions of enormous cloud banks drifted overhead. Somewhere to the west he saw the reflections of sheet lightning, a flicker through dark mist it meant the lightning was somewhere beyond a thick haze of falling rain.

Provo had picked the most exposed spot on the map to camp. Shelby huddled in the chill night and tried to see out across the meadows. Menendez was sitting up on the far side of camp, by the horses, watching that way. The grass was cropped down short—Navajo sheep had grazed it and moved on. There wasn't a tree for half a mile in any direction. The flat dish of grass was surrounded by mountainsides. A creek came down out of the peaks and ran along the lower end of the meadow before it spilled over a waterfall into a canyon beyond; the creek-bank trees, maybe a thousand yards away, were the nearest cover of any kind. Shelby felt isolated, exposed, and nervous, even though he knew there wasn't a rifleman alive who could make a bullet count at that range.

They had come down into the meadow by a roundabout switchbacking route. When Provo had chosen the campsite, out in the middle of the grass, Gant had exploded in anger. Provo had ignored him completely: the only remark he made was, 'Rivers can be as changeable as women. That creek's changed its course some since last time I was here.'

Portugee had yelled and bitched. It was a setup for an ambush. They could be surrounded. It was a trap. Menendez had laughed at him. Provo had said, 'Only two men after us. How's two men going to surround anybody?'

Shelby knew he was right. It made perfect sense. Burgade couldn't come within range of them without showing himself on the meadow. There was no cover. But what the hell did Provo intend to prove by all this?

And there was another worry. He could already begin to make out the vague shadow-streaks of falling rain above the slopes immediately to the west, illuminated by frequent bursts of lightning. In a few minutes the storm would be on top of them. It could conceal Burgade if he came then.

Shelby unfolded his oilskin slicker and put his head through the poncho hole. He laced it up around his throat and sat with the poncho flowing around him, a tent that covered him from the neck down. He stared into the cool opaque night with wide eyes and kept shifting his grip on the rifle. Once, he thought he saw something move in the corner of his vision; he whipped his head around and stared. Nothing. He swallowed and glanced across at where Menendez was sitting, but he could no longer make out Menendez's shape in the impenetrable black.

He knew his fear was irrational. They were eight against two — or anyhow seven against two; Weed hadn't come back yet, but nobody expected him before dawn. But groundless or not, fear was a constriction against which Shelby pushed with increasing resentment.

The drumming crash of the thunderstorm awoke the others; there were rustlings and stirrings, men wrapping themselves in oilskins. Shelby walked over to where Susan Burgade lay. Provo had tied her hands behind her and hobbled her ankles. Someone had thrown an oilskin across her. Shelby couldn't tell if she was awake. She didn't stir when he bent down over her. He straightened up after awhile and walked back to his post.

There was rain. It came down hard and sudden, as if dumped out of buckets from treetop height. Fierce lightning licked across the sky in fragments and stabbed towards the earth, brought down by metal in the mountain rocks. Inside of a minute the water was runneling out of the trough of Shelby's hatbrim, dripping down the back of his neck, getting inside the collar of the slicker. Within a few more minutes he was soaked through.

'Easy, Mike. It's me.'

Provo's voice made him jump a foot off the ground. Shelby turned and said, 'Christ, Zach.'

'Can't see anything in this rain anyway. Let's you and me go sit with missy.'

'She's all right. I just checked her.'

'I know. But Burgade might take a notion to come in tonight, use the rain for cover. If he does, he'll try to find his girl and ease her out of here without us seeing him.

Shelby went with him to the girl. She hadn't moved. Provo didn't sit down. He stood above the girl, a tall lean shadow in flowing oilskins. Shelby sat down on the wet ground and brooded miserably into the rain. A shaft of lightning sizzled down not half a mile away and thunder crashed immediately. The rain was a steady splashing racket.

The waiting rubbed his nerves. He tried to occupy himself by making plans, thinking about the gold, deciding step by step where he would go and what he would do. Australia, he thought. Or East Africa. Ride from here up across the Four Corners into the Rockies. Get outfitted in respectable clothes in Ouray or Silverton, so he wouldn't attract attention. They probably had his picture on post office walls, but he had an ordinary young face, likely nobody'd spot him if he just used his head, kept calm, didn't act like a fugitive. Ride the coach on up through Grand Junction and up into the Jackson Hole country. Up past the Tetons through Cody, on up by Butte and Helena and right through into Canada. If the money looked short he'd knock over a country store or two, but do it at night and wear a mask so nobody'd see his face. Keep moving, that was the trick. As long as you kept moving and didn't shackle yourself to anybody else, you'd be all right. Loners always had the best chance because there was nobody to betray them.

That was why it bothered him staying here. He didn't want to rely on Provo or anybody else; and he didn't like standing still like this. But he'd invested his time and he had the money coming to him. He was going to stick it out until Provo came across with the gold. And Provo would. There wasn't going to be any double-cross. Not with seven of them against Provo. If he got balky about leading them to the gold, they'd make him talk. Provo was tough, all right, but no man alive was *that* tough.

Burgade didn't show up. Neither did Weed. At dawn the sky was dark and wild, but the rain had moved on. There was no reason not to build a fire since they weren't hiding any longer, but there was no dry wood to be had and Provo vetoed it when Riva and Quesada volunteered to go over to the trees and hunt around for covered fuel. 'Why take a chance of getting picked off when you can stay out here safe?'

So they ate cold breakfasts and let the clothes dry on their backs. Susan Burgade sat huddled and dull-eyed, her long hair matted and damp. Shelby gave her something to eat and she pushed it around the plate. She didn't have any interest in it, but when Shelby came back after twenty minutes to get the plate and scour it out, she'd finished it all. Reflex, probably; she had a vacant look on her face and probably didn't even remember having eaten.

The sun burned off the ground-water, which had clung to the grass like dew. By ten in the morning it was as if there hadn't been a rain at all. Riva was fussing over the horses. The rest of them sat around or wandered about on foot, kicking at the ground and brooding and building up nervous impatience. Selby could tell nobody was going to put up with this for long. Weed hadn't returned and everybody was speculating about what might have happened to him, but finally Provo put a stop to the guesses.

'You all know damn well what happened to him. He wasn't smart enough. Burgade set a trap and George walked into it. We won't be seeing George anymore. Forget him. We didn't need him anyway.'

Provo stood a little distance from the rest of them. He was in his shirtsleeves, hatless, the wind blowing through his raven-black hair. He had a rifle in both hands, not pointed anywhere in particular but ready for use. 'Let's don't fool around,' he said. 'I know what you're thinking. A little mutiny in mind. You don't like sitting around here right out in bare-ass daylight and not doing anything. You want to grab your gold and go. All right, I don't blame you for that, but we made a bargain and I kept my part of it. I kept you out of the hands of the law. Now you're going to keep your part of it. You're going to help me punch Sam Burgade's ticket for the promised land. As soon as that's done, you'll get your gold and you can go.'

Mike Shelby said slowly, 'Listen, Zach, I can't talk for anybody else, but the way I see it, either we get Burgade quick or we forget it. Burgade's already got one man riding with him, we saw them yesterday. It won't be but a few days before the law boys bust through that handy Navajo red-tape of yours and come swarmin' on to the Reservation. Another three, four days up here and we'll be boxed in like steers in a slaughter-house. What if Burgade just sits out there and watches us until his reinforcements show up?'

Provo's iron eyes narrowed when his lips smiled. 'I'll make you a bargain, Mike. All of you. If we don't bring Burgade down by tomorrow sundown, I'll point you to the gold and you can go dig it up and be on your way. That sound fair to everybody? Any objections?'

A group of them stood in a knot — Gant, Shiraz, Quesada, Riva. They talked swiftly among themselves. Shelby stood off to the side, near Menendez. Shelby didn't join in the discussion but he said to Provo, 'Satisfies me, I guess.'

Provo said, 'Portugee, the rest of you — one other little treat in the package for you. Two or three of you been wanting to have a hack at missy, here.'

Will Gant tugged at his nostril hair. 'You fixin' to let us have her?'

'When the time comes.'

'When'll that be?' When Gant looked at Susan Burgade his neck swelled with musky desire. She must have been aware of it — she was looking right at him — but there was no break in her dull, indifferent expression.

'It'll be when I say it's to be,' Provo said. 'Take it or leave it, Will.'

Portugee punched Gant in the arm. 'Aw, hell with it, Will. We gone along this far with him.'

Gant sat down slowly on the pile of saddles. He put his hands on his knees. The weight of his huge belly sagged against his thighs. He smiled.

Shelby was standing close by when Menendez walked over and said to Provo, 'Listen, Zach, what if Weed ef-fell off some focking cleef last night and bosted his es-stupid neck? What if Burgade never got him at all? That rain las' night washed out our tracks for es-sure.'

'You're saying you're worried Burgade won't find us?'

'Ahjess. The sonoma bitch, he's old, Zach, and he's es-scared, and maybe he's all focked up and not thinking es-straight.'

Provo laughed without humour. 'He's stuck to us this far like a burr under a blanket. Don't underestimate Sam Burgade. He's not a son of a bitch, Menendez, he's *the* son of a bitch, but that doesn't make him a fool. He knows where we are. Or if he doesn't, he'll find us soon enough.'

'Maybe. But we ain't got jost a whole lot of time. Why not make es-sure, Zach? Why not es-send him an eenvitation?'

Provo squinted at the sun as if to judge the time. 'Maybe you got a point,' he said. He lifted his voice and bellowed 'Hey, all of you. I'm going to fire a few shots. Don't anybody get nervous. Riva, take care of those horses, see they don't spook from the noise.'

Gant said, 'What the hell?'

The last of his words was drowned in the rolling thunder of Provo's revolver. He was shooting indifferently into the earth ten yards from his feet. The bullets ploughed up spouts of dirt. The noise echoed across the flats. 'That ought to bring him,' Provo said mildly, and opened the revolver to plug out the empties and reload.

Provo repeated the noisemaking every hour or so for the rest of the morning and into the early afternoon. Every time he did it, it took Riva and Quesada and Shelby a good ten or fifteen minutes to calm down the hobbled horses. The horses had never been trained to guns. It was a good thing they hadn't had any running gunfights on these animals.

Susan Burgade sat like a stone until two in the afternoon. Provo spent most of his time scanning the surrounding timber fringe through his spyglass, sitting on the ground and studying each quadrant with great and patient care before he shifted his seat to survey the next. Obviously looking for signs of Burgade.

About two o'clock Provo went over to the girl. Shelby was near enough to hear him say, 'Get up and walk around some, missy. You don't want to get a cramp in your legs from sitting all day.'

Susan didn't argue. She didn't even seem to resent the command. She got up and walked back and forth like some kind of mechanism. The wind spun her hair around her face; she combed it away with her fingers and tossed it back with a shake of her head. She had good long legs and a practical stride. There was nothing alive in her face but her eyes, which were full of thinly guarded panic.

Shelby watched her walk back and forth and thought how lovely she was, even with her filthy wrinkled clothes, even with dirt on her face and in her hair. He didn't much like what Provo was doing. Getting her up and walking her around was a way of telling Sam Burgade the bait was still alive. Provo had to assume Burgade was out there somewhere in the trees, probably watching through field glasses. Maybe he was and maybe he wasn't. Shelby didn't like any of it.

Will Gant came along and stopped beside Shelby to watch the girl with his crude sensual leer. He was watching her buttocks as she walked. 'Oh, Jesus,' Gant whispered in awe. 'Oh, Jesus H. Christ, will you look at that.'

Gant's breath made Shelby turn away. The sun was high and hot. A trickle of sweat ran out of his armpit, down his ribs.

Along about half past three, Provo suddenly stopped his telescope-watching and got to his feet. 'He's out there,' he said positively. 'Over east in those oaks and cedars. I caught a flash, must have been the lens of his glass.'

Shelby said, 'What do we do now?'

Porgugee Shiraz said, 'Hell, we ought to wait for dark and set up a fucking ambush a fly couldn't get through.'

Shelby was dubious. Night ambushes could work two ways. He turned to speak, but Provo cut him off: 'No. Why play at his game? All we need to do is wait for him to come to us.'

Shelby said, 'He can wait us out. He's got more time than we've got.'

Provo seemed amused — genuinely amused for the first time since the breakout. 'Well, in that case, let's give him a little entertainment to help him pass the time. Missy? You don't mind, come along here with me.'

Provo took Susan's arm. She didn't shake him off. He steered her up past the horses on to the little rise of grass, only thirty feet beyond camp. 'Sit yourself down, missy. You want to wave to your old man over there? Go ahead. Wave to him.'

She sat down and put her hands in her lap. Provo laughed. 'Suit yourself.' He turned and lifted his voice. 'The old man's got a box-seat view. Will, Portugee, you two been aching to dip your wicks. Now's your time. Come on up here and have your fun.'

Stunned and horror-struck, Shelby could feel the sudden anger rising in him, the coming explosion. Heat rushed to his face. '*No!*' he roared. He locked his fist over the grip of his holstered revolver. He stood facing Gant and Portugee.

Provo's abrasive baritone shot forward. 'Let them by, Mike.'

'The hell.' He didn't look over his shoulder at Provo. 'You got no call to do this to her. She never did you any grief.'

'Mike, I won't mess around with you. You make trouble now and you'll be mostly a hole.'

The voice was dead-flat. Shelby turned slowly to look. Provo had his rifle across the crook of his elbow, pointed generally at him. Shelby trembled in rage.

Gant and Portugee began to walk up past him. Sunlight raced along Provo's rifle in a fragmented glitter of darting reflections. Gant and Portugee drew their holster-guns and dropped them on the ground as they walked past; Gant was muttering: '... wipe that touch-me-not look off that high and mighty face of hers.' Gant had a rancid smell. He walked heavily on his heels, undoing his belt. Shelby saw the spittle running from his mouth. He wore an expression of anger rather than lust.

Portugee was breathing fast. His urgent need showing in his trousers. Gant, hot in the face, walked up and dropped his trousers and stood staring at Susan. Gant held his erection in his hand.

Susan sat frozen with dread, sweating, quivering in every rigid limb.

Quesada shouldered past Shelby and went up the slope after them. 'I want a piece of this.'

Menendez looked on with sneering contempt. Taco Riva refused to watch: he turned his back and began savagely currying one of the horses. Shelby stood rooted, drenched in sweat and rage.

Will Gant said, 'You first, Portugee. I want to watch.'

Portugee didn't even take down his pants. He just opened his fly and dropped to his knees. He put his hand on Susan's breast and smiled.

Susan closed her eyes. She sagged to the ground, drawn up like a sick, aged wreck. Shelby couldn't even tell if she was conscious.

Provo wasn't even watching them. Provo was watching Shelby. The gun was rock steady in Provo's hands. Shelby's fingernails cut into his palms.

Portugee ripped Susan's shirt open and kneaded her breasts brutally. He was going to take her roughly, as if to reassure himself he was the equal of any other man. He shoved her back against the earth and Shelby heard him say, 'Spread her legs out and hold her feet down.' Quesada did it.

Suddenly the girl moved. She made a grab for a knife in Portugee's belt scabbard. She got it out and whipped it towards his belly.

The tip drew blood. Portugee snapped both hands around her wrist and twisted in opposite directions. The knife fell from her hand and Shelby heard her suck wind in through her teeth. Her head rocked back and her eyes rolled back in her head. Shelby saw her go limp and knew she had lost consciousness.

It didn't stop them.

CHAPTER TEN

BURGADE lay on the ground stunned. His head thundered with pain. He opened his eyes to slits. Light streamed down through the trees, its colour very rich.

He saw Hal fingering the field glasses in his lap. They trembled in Hal's hands. Breath hissed and sawed in and out of him. 'I can't look, either,' Hal said. His face was a twisted ugly mask of anguish and fury.

Burgade wiped his sleeve across his eyes. He rolled over and made a grab for the rifle.

Hal planted his foot on Burgade's wrist. 'No, sir. I don't want to hit you again.'

'You should have let me shoot.'

'You might have hit Susan. At this range you can't — '

'Then let me get closer! In God's name, man —'

'There's no God,' Hal said. 'Not out there.'

Burgade struggled to free his wrist. Hal reached out and picked up the rifle. 'No. There's seven of them.'

'Leave me alone!'

'Sir,' Hal said, his voice shaking, 'that's what they *want.*'

'Then let them have it!' He jerked his arm free and rolled over.

Hal jumped him, pinned him to the ground. 'Get hold of yourself. They haven't killed her.'

Burgade lay with his face pinned against the ground. A twig dug into his cheek. He heard the rasp of his own breathing. The pulse thudded in his throat. Hal said in a soft hiss, with calculated brutality, 'Women have been fucked before. She can survive it if we can.'

Through the red haze of grief and unthinking total anger, Burgade felt a twinge of awe that this young man, who loved her, could take it so coolly.

His eyes brimmed: he wept.

'Are you all right now?'

'Yes.'

Hal let him up. He sat up and wiped dirt and leaves off himself numbly. 'What are they doing now?'

'Nothing.'

'What about Susan?'

'She's lying where they left her. I don't think she knew what they were doing. I think she fainted. It's just as well.'

Burgade reached for the field glasses. 'Is she — '

'She's got her clothes on, what's left of them. And I'm sure she's not hurt. I saw her move.'

'Not hurt.'

'You know what I mean, sir. She's alive. That's what it comes down to, isn't it? In the end. Staying alive is what matters.'

'You're a tougher son of a bitch than I ever credited.'

'Yes, sir, I guess I am.'

Burgade spent a long time looking through the field glasses. They had an eight-power magnification but still that only brought the camp up to a hundred yards' distance; he couldn't make out details. He saw Susan roll over on her side and draw her knees up. One of the men was standing nearby. He couldn't tell for certain, but by the set of the man's head and the movements of his hands it appeared he was talking to Susan, trying to calm her down. It wasn't Provo. After a long time, eliminating names, he finally decided it had to be Shelby, the kid. He didn't know whether Shelby was one of the ones who had raped her. He'd seen Gant drop his pants and then he had flung down the field glasses in disbelieving rage. He'd reached for the rifle in a blind savage fury and Hal had knocked him down.

He put down the glasses and took half a dozen evenly spaced deep breaths, with his eyes closed. Finally he looked at Hal. 'Thank you.'

Hal was very grave. 'Yes, sir. I couldn't let you do it. I felt the same way you did. But they'd have killed you. And I can't help her, without you. I wouldn't know what to do. I can help, but you've got to point the way for me.'

'You don't need a weathervane, Hal. You're a better man than you think you are.'

'I know my limitations, sir. My ignorances. What I don't know about this kind of thing would fill an encyclopaedia.' Hal's glance turned outward, past the trees towards the flat. In a different voice he said, 'We're going to get her out of this, sir. You and me. And when we do I'm going to try to make her see that this hasn't made any difference in the way I feel. It's going to take a long time and a lot of patience. From you and from me. She's going to have to travel a long road back before she can trust a man's hands again — mine or any other man's.'

Burgade stared at him and listened to the quiet run of Hal's talk. Suddenly feeling almost burst his throat. He grabbed Hal around the shoulders and hugged him against him and felt the tears wet on his cheeks.

The sun was painful against his grainy eyes. He shaded his brow and studied the sky across and beyond the flats, above the westward summits. He felt utterly drained, It took a supreme effort just to lower his hand to his side. The ground around his feet was still damp, saturated by last night's pelting rain; the topsoil among these trees was thin, the rock and clay beneath it wasn't porous, and there was no place for the water to go. But the grass out on the flats had been dried by the day's blast of sunshine.

It would work. He turned and began to walk back through the trees to the clearing where they had tethered the horses. Weed was there, tied to the bole of an oak, a bandanna gag in his mouth. His face was swollen on one side where Burgade had struck him last night; the eye was puffy and half-closed. He looked bitter.

While Hal fed Weed and gave him water, Burgade squatted with two boxes of rifle cartridges in his lap and the pair of wirecutter pliers that every horseman carried in his kit. They weren't made for this kind of work but they'd do. He used them to work the lead bullets out of each cartridge. He poured the powder into one of the empty cartridge boxes and when he was through with his methodical chore he had a little more than half a boxful of gunpowder.

The sun was settling towards the horizon. Hal said, 'You've got something in mind.'

Burgade grunted. 'There's a steady westerly breeze across that meadow. Comes right down off those canyons on the far side. I don't think it'll shift for a while. We're going to have a clear night — that storm blew the clouds over. Quarter moon comes up about ten o'clock. It won't be too bad a light for shooting.'

'But we can't go crawling out there, sir. They'd see us easy, against all that pale yellow grass.'

'We're not going to them, Hal. They're coming to me.'

Hal nodded towards the box of powder. 'That's got something to do with it, of course?'

'Yes. You've got a watch, haven't you?'

'Yes, sir.'

'All right. It'll be dark in an hour or so. I want you to take this powder and ride around to the far side of the meadow, down at the bottom — directly opposite where we are now. Circle wide when you go, don't take chances, and don't hurry, there's plenty of time. Tie your horse well back in the trees over there and come down to the edge of timber on foot. The wind will be behind you. You'll get there about nine o'clock, my judgment. The moon won't be up yet. Stay in the shadows under the front line of trees there, and spread a thin line of this gunpowder along the edge of the grass, as long as you can make it without gaps. It doesn't need to be more than a quarter of an inch wide — just a thin ribbon of powder. Then gather up whatever dry kindling you can find and scatter it along there in the grass. The moon will come up, and we'll need to have it high, so you'll wait until half past midnight. Got it?'

'Twelve thirty. Yes, sir.'

'Take these matches,' Burgade said. He handed Hal the oilskin pouch. 'At half past midnight, post yourself at the centre of the line of gunpowder. Then wait for the wind. As soon as you've got a fair breeze blowing, touch a match to the powder.'

'In other words, set fire to the grass.'

'Yes. A grass fire will go like hell. It burns low to the ground and makes its own wind as it goes — whips along so fast it won't even consume the leaves of trees it goes under. It'll explode across that meadow.'

'I see. And drive Provo this way.'

'On foot. They won't be able to handle those horses once they smell smoke.'

'Do you think Susan will — '

'That's what I'm here for,' Burgade said. 'I'll get her away from them in the confusion if I possibly can.'

'And if you can't ?'

'If I can't we'll still be better off than we are now. They'll be up here in the trees where we can get close to them.'

'Yes, sir,' Hal said. 'And what then? The reason I'm asking — well, if anything — '

'I know. If anything happens to me you'll want to know what to do next.'

'I meant no offence.'

'It's no time for politeness,' Burgade muttered. 'If we can't get Susan away from them tonight, I can't think of but one thing left to do, and it's not a thing I expect you to approve.'

'Approve? To hell with that. I'm changing a lot of my notions.'

'Then pick them off one by one.'

'Tall order, sir.'

'Yes. It is.'

Hal sucked air through his teeth.

Burgade said, 'One more thing. Him.' He inclined his head towards George Weed. 'When you go around to set the fire, take him with you.'

'What for?'

'We don't want the rest of them tripping over him and

turning him loose, do we. It'd only add another gun against us.'

Hal picked up the powder box and weighted it in his hand. His face was deeply trenched by exhaustion. Dark sweat-circles stained the armpits of his shirt. 'I feel as if it's all a puking rotten dream and I'm never going to wake up from it. We're talking calmly about killing seven men.'

'My only regret,' Burgade breathed in answer, 'is that I can only kill Zach Provo once.'

Burgade looked up. Oak branches were silhouetted against the sky, colourless and jagged like cracks in porcelain. His eyes felt sticky: he was taut as a watch spring, ready to snap. The picketed horses stirred. He heard the light thud of a hoof, the swish of a tail. 'Time for you to go. Put Weed on my horse. I won't have a use for a horse tonight.'

'Won't you need one for Susan?'

'We'll have a better chance on foot. Horse makes too much noise.' Burgade walked him over to the animals and helped him cinch them up. His weary muscles throbbed with pain; there was a steady, maddening tremor in his old hands. Even in the dim starlight he could see the ridged dark veins along the backs of his wrists. He said, 'As soon as the fire's burning, ride well around back. Don't try to mix into whatever may be going on down here — you might shoot me, or get shot by me. Just go on up to that creek where we camped last night. Think you can find it again?'

'Yes, sir.'

'If I can get Susan away, that's where I'll take her. If we don't appear by sunrise you'll have to use your own judgment.' He turned and grasped Hal's elbow. 'When you come back across, swing wide and take it very slow. You don't want to fall into any traps. Better leave Weed over there — he'd only clutter things up, and we need the horse more than we need him.'

'I don't know — what if nobody comes across him? He could die out there, tied up.'

'Let him.' Burgade tightened his grip on Hal's arm. 'Our lives are more important than his. Important to Susan. I don't care if Weed lives or dies.'

Hal shook his head slowly. 'I know he's asked for it. But just the same — '

'We'll pick him up if we can.'

He felt Hal loosen up; he dropped his hand away. Hal said, 'I guess I know you're right, sir, but it's a hell of a thing to have to do.'

'I know.'

Hal's eyes came up. 'Look, you be careful too.'

'I don't intend to let them get at me until I've finished what we came here to do.'

'Susan's going to need you, sir. It may not matter to you if they kill you in the end. But it matters to her. You understand what I'm saying?'

Burgade turned away. 'Let's get Weed on his horse.'

He picked a spot with care. At first he thought of climbing a tree to get a better command of the meadow. But he was too weak. And even if he could get himself up into one of the oaks, he'd be lucky to get down again without snapping his brittle bones.

He chose a fallen dead tree just inside the edge of the forest. Sat down on the deadfall trunk and arranged his rifle and field glasses at hand. From here he could see the whole meadow.

After the moon came up he fixed his field glasses on the camp and kept watch through the ticking silence of the night. There was always the chance Provo would decide to move.

He kept thinking about what Hal had said. From the beginning of the chase he had resigned himself; he had not expected to come out alive. He hadn't much cared. They could have his old used-up hide, if that was the price of Susan's life. But there was a chance. Hal was right: if this thing hadn't broken her, destroyed her beyond repair, it had come close. She would need gentle patience, protective love. His own death might mean nothing to him; to her it might be the final injury, and too much for her gentle spirit to accept all at once.

There had been nothing beyond Susan's rescue and vengeance upon Provo. An old man, fit for nothing but a slow bitter draining of final years in the Pioneers' Home — guttering out, in the end, like the noxious stub of a used-up candle. It occurred to him that a part of him had wanted to end it clean, up here in the high country that was unchanged from forty years ago: to make a last valiant fight of it, take Provo with him, go out in a hysterical blaze of glorious violence: a far more fitting finish for Sam Burgade. Storybook ending, high tragedy.

An indulgence, he saw now. A cheap poetic fantasy. An old man's pathetic dream, images of William S. Hart meeting a Shakespearean death in the last reel.

A corner of his vanity resented Hal's wisdom. Hal, clear-eyed and sensible, had destroyed the dream.

But Hal had replaced it with something important. *She'll need me*, he thought. The wonder of it made his old hands steady, made his jaw creep forward to lie in a hard line. *She'll need me.*

How long had it been since anybody had needed Sam Burgade?

He sat there for hours, shifting his buttocks on the hard wood. Wind-stirred leaves made moving shadows along the moonlit ground. He kept checking his watch at close intervals and when it went past midnight he began to hear the beat of his own heart. The light seemed to grow brighter, every tiny sound louder. He played the field glasses over the pale silver meadow and his eyeballs seemed to scrape the sockets.

He'd told Hal half past midnight. Five minutes ahead of the appointed moment he picked up the ·06 Springfield and jacked the bolt halfway open to make sure a cartridge was chambered in the breech. He snicked the safety off and hunched himself forward with his elbows on his knees, wrapping himself around the rifle like a 'possum, holding the field glasses in one hand in such a way that he could drop them instantly and bring the rifle to bear in the same brief movement.

He heard crickets in the trees. Sweat prickled his scalp, breaking out like needles.

In the eight-power lenses he could see the horses plainly, the prone shapes of half a dozen figures, and two men sitting up with rifles, at opposite sides of the camp. One of them got up, restless, and walked back and forth.

The air was quite still. He'd told Hal to wait for a wind. His hands sweated and he wiped them one at a time on his trousers, and levelled the rifle again, locked it in tight in a marksman's grip. The steel butt plate was cold through his clothing against his bony shoulder.

The cropped grass began to ripple, long silver glimmers like ocean swell. He locked the field glasses against the bridge of his nose and stared until his eyes ached. The breeze stirred his hair where it curled out under the hatbrim.

Abruptly, through the glasses, he saw a thin ribbon-stripe of light burst into sight at the bottom of the meadow. It looked like the crack of light under a closed door: trees and mountains grew darker behind it. It spread with a rush.

The pacing sentry stood bolt still. Burgade saw his shoulders lift when he filled his chest with air to give the alarm The shout was thin in the distance. Figures on the ground began to stir.

The fire blasted forward like whitewater cascades. Unsteady winds spread it wider and wider. It raced forward, gathering brightness, throwing diamond sparks; whipped along, low to the ground and vicious.

Several men in camp were on their feet. It took them time to realise what was happening. Voices of surprise and querulous discovery rode the wind. Burgade held the glasses in rock-steady hands. He had them silhouetted against the fire now: he began to sort them out. He was looking for Susan.

The low racing blaze licked out at both sides, hungry for fuel, making its own hot wind now: rolling smoke shot forward from the crest. The fire's heat expanded the air around it, accelerating the flames, turning them blue-yellow. Spreading like poured oil, it flashed out past its own edges, widening the swath — within seconds it covered half the width of the lower meadow. With quick fury it consumed its sparse spindly fuel and raced on to find more.

The camp was in panic. One man — it had to be Riva — had gone running towards the horses. Four or five of them were rearing and plunging. Riva dodged in among them, bent low in a crouch Burgade caught the quick flash of light along an oustretched blade — Riva was cutting the hobbles. One by one the terrified horses leaped away and bolted forward until there were only three left. Evidently the three had not been unsaddled. Riva had them by the reins, he was fighting to keep them still. Out there, by now, the smell of smoke must be powerful. Burgade's own nose caught a hint of it. Through the high-resolution lenses he saw two or three men break for it, running up on foot, not towards Burgade but off at an angle that would bring them into the trees two hundred yards to his right. He focused the glasses on them long enough to make sure Susan was not among them, and swung the glasses back.

Riva was with the horses, climbing up into a saddle, shouting something. The horses were dancing, rearing; nobody ran towards Riva, and after a brief moment more, Riva spurred the horse he was riding and led the other two horses away with him at a dead gallop, heading directly towards Burgade. Behind Riva, three men were moving across the camp on foot, starkly outlined against the flames. Zach Provo's clawed praying-mantis silhouette was unmistakable. Burgade sucked breath sharply into his lungs. Then, for a brief instant, he glimpsed Susan — on her feet, running. She'd been hidden from his sight behind the horses.

But now Riva came veering forward, cutting off Burgade's view of the camp: the three horses loomed heavy in the field glasses. Riva was drumming straight towards him, high and sharp-shouldered in the saddle.

He had to get those horses out of his line of sight. He

braced the Springfield against his shoulder and dropped the glasses; took aim with deliberate care and fired, at four hundred yards.

Wherever the bullet went, it missed its target. Burgade racked the bolt open and slammed it shut, settled his aim and squeezed like a target-range shooter, not breathing, not closing either eye. When the Springfield went off it surprised him, as it should: and Riva threw up his arms and pitched back off his horse.

Freed, the three horses scattered in panic. Burgade fumbled for the glasses at his feet. The fire swarmed across the width of the meadow, crowding up with savage speed. The low angle of view made it hard to tell how close it was to the camp. Three of the men had run up towards the timber at Burgade's right; they were almost into the trees now but he didn't waste attention on them. One of the loose horses ran into the trees and he heard it crashing around. He could taste smoke now. He swung the field glasses to bear on the camp—the flames had almost reached it: but the four figures hadn't begun to run for it.

Susan was out there. Burgade's eyes went wide. He saw Provo shouting, making gestures. Provo had a grip on Susan's wrist. She was trying to run; Provo held her back. Burgade hardly spared the two other men a glance; he didn't care who they were. He saw Provo bend down and butt his shoulder against Susan's midriff and straighten up with Susan across his back in a fireman's carry, one arm across the backs of her knees; carrying her like that, Provo turned and ran back towards the other two men. The fire rushed forward, obscuring things in smoke, but Burgade caught fragmentary images: the three men wheeling through the smoke, jogging away from him—

—*Provo was running into the fire!*

In that sudden split moment of time he knew. Provo had not panicked. Provo had judged the speed of the flames, the sparse grass it fed on. Provo knew the fire had been set to drive him up this way. And Provo hadn't fallen for it. Provo was going *through* the fire—he would break out of it, behind it, and run across the burned earth into the trees beyond.

He had a brief glimpse of one of them leaping high, running desperately, boots plunging through the low flames. Then they were gone — through and beyond, hidden from him by the blaze.

His eyes stared without believing. The whipping flames rushed forward — smoke began to burn his throat. His eyes started to water. *Got to think. Get a grip.* His head jerked around to the right — three of them had gone into the trees up that way. Possibly they'd seen the muzzle-flame of his rifle, shooting Riva down. He had to move away from this spot, keep from being ambushed. He swung his feet over the deadfall and went swiftly back deeper into the forest, lugging the Springfield and the glasses. He kept moving uphill; the low white moon ran along with him, above the treetops.

Out of breath, he stopped on a slope and looked down. Through the trees he could see the fire's tail whip around, curling towards the trees off to the left. It would hit the rain-logged ground and the damp floor of the forest, and burn itself out against that moisture; not much chance of a forest fire catching. He searched the lower woods for movement. There was a good chance of picking it up against the firelight beyond.

He saw movement in two or three places but inspection proved it was only Riva's horses, dashing around in fear. Burgade leaned against a tree and gulped wind. His chest heaved, his leg muscles trembled. *Think.*

Provo had got away with Susan. Over on the far side. Instinct urged him to get over there as fast as he could and get after them, But a cooler second thought stopped him. No good to go after Provo with these three over here behind him. They might spot him, rig a crossfire. No. The thing to do was take these three out of the fight first. The fire had separated them from Provo. Fear would be working on them. They wouldn't be thinking about Provo, or Susan, or even Provo's gold. They'd be thinking about flight. Afraid of hidden guns in the dark forest. Get away from here — that was what they'd want.

Flight meant horses. Those three would be coming down this way, where Riva's horses had entered the trees. They'd come not for Burgade but for the horses.

That was it, then. Get close to the horses and wait for the men to come. Burgade nodded. His breath had evened out. He began to work his way down through the timber.

The horses were easy to follow. Innate herd-habit had drawn them together and they made plenty of noise, banging around in the trees. As soon as they had got beyond smell of the smoke they had begun to calm down. When Burgade caught up with them they were moving slowly through the forest, starting to browse leaves and grass tufts. Three were saddled. In a short while they began to mill. He counted six, and that gave him pause: there had been nine to begin with — the other three had drifted off in some other direction, or Provo's men had captured them. In the latter case, it meant no one would be coming after these six horses. Not for quite a while, at least.

The chances were diminishing: he cursed the shift, but there was no point speculating about those missing three horses. He'd picked his strategy; now he had to play it out. If nobody came looking for the horses in an hour or so, he'd have to try something else, but in the meantime — *Lord Jesus!*

He wheeled on his feet and stared back the way he had come. *Of all the fool stupid things to do . . .* The ground here on the hill was still dew-damp from last night's downpour. His own tracks, superimposed over the prints of the idling horses, were clear for anybody to follow. *Right out in front of God and everybody. You're getting senile.*

Well, he could hardly try to wipe them out, he'd only be obscuring the horse prints too.

He was old, he was dead tired, and it took him four or five minutes standing there in the silence to figure out what thirty years ago he'd have done instinctively. It left him profoundly depressed, more so than before, because now for the first time he felt the crawl of uncertainty in him as his self-confidence, which was the one thing that had kept him going, began to drain. He had pumped himself full of arrogance: now all of a sudden he was allowing himself to realise how poor his chances really were — of getting near Provo at all, of getting Susan away, of even staying alive through the next six hours.

He knew what to do to solve the immediate problem. The knowledge didn't cheer him, because it had taken him such a long sluggish time to work it out in his head. Provo wasn't going to give him that kind of time. So he did what had to be done, but he did it without heart. He kept on walking boldly ahead until he was within a few yards of the horses and they had stopped grazing to peer at him in spooky suspicion. Then, where one of the horses had stood and churned up the ground a little as if waiting for a rider to get mounted, he dug his right boot-toe deep into the earth, to leave a sharp toe-print of the kind that might have been left by a man putting his left foot into a stirrup and pushing himself up on his right tiptoe to get mounted

Then he backtracked, carefully. Walked backwards in his own tracks, careful to put his weight on his heels. He backed up until he was beside a mossy patch of rocks. Stepped to one side on to the rocks, leaving no tracks, and faded back into the woods, walking on brush and deadwood, leaving no sign that a casual eye would discern. He circled close in alongside the track again and posted himself at a crouch, hidden from the trail by heavy bushes and tree trunks, but within three or four feet of the line of his own footprints. He cradled the rifle and waited for them to come.

He was counting on the three of them coming together — not in a tight-packed bunch, but spread out behind one another for mutual protection. But it would work as well if fewer than three came; it would only mean he would then have to find whoever hadn't come this way, and that would take longer. He was up against the factor of time, partly because time would fray Provo's nerves, partly because he himself needed sleep badly and could not go much longer without.

He didn't trust his old brain, he worked it out step by step in his mind to make sure he had not made some stupid mistake. Assume all three of them came, looking for the horses. In the moonlight they wouldn't have counted the number of horses by the tracks; they wouldn't know whether there had been six horses or seven. They would come along here, following the tracks, following Burgade's bootprints. The bootprints would make them wary and they'd be spread out quite wide of each other, but at least one of them would be on this trail. Or they'd be single file, separated. In the former case he'd jump the nearest one and try to put him away silently, without alarming the others. In the latter case he'd let the first two go by and then jump the third one, then close in behind the other two while they reached the sudden end of his bootprints. They would assume Burgade had mounted one of the horses and ridden away on it; by the time they spotted the fact that there were no hoofprints leading away from the six remaining horses, Burgade hoped to be on top of them.

It seemed foolproof enough. It was the only kind of thing you could do when you were one against three: divide them, pick them off one at a time.

But he was scared.

His nerves kept playing tricks on him. The two .30-06 shots he'd fired at Taco Riva had left his ears blocked, there was still a ringing in his skull, and he wasn't confident he would hear them before they were very close. He wasn't sure he was agile enough to jump a man from a brush-ambush like this and get to the man before the man heard him coming. He wasn't sure of a lot of things. He hid and waited and trembled with fear.

They were a little careless, and he heard their twig-snapping approach. Three of them. They were coming up through the forest, walking together. Then, about seventy-five feet downslope from him, they stopped and discussed things. He couldn't hear their words. In the shadowy moonlight under the trees he couldn't be sure of all of them, but two of them were very big men, one of them had a lot of meat on him, and that one had to be Will Gant. The other big one was probably Joaquim Quesada. The third man, leaner, might be Menendez or it might be Shiraz or it could even be the kid, Shelby; impossible to tell.

He saw now why they had paused. They were standing at just about the point where Burgade's tracks came down off the hillside and turned to follow the prints of the horses.

One of them — Gant made arm gestures, and the smallest of the three turned off into the woods and went downhill, west, disappearing into the trees. Burgade couldn't see whether that one carried a rifle or not. Anyhow the man seemed to be working in a half circle, probably intending to come up on the horses from one side.

Now Gant began to walk forward, leaving Quesada back there to cover him. Gant came right along on top of Burgade's prints, moving swiftly from tree to tree, taking his time to keen the night at each pause. They could as easily have turned around and gone away, but that wasn't the way their minds would work. They would figure they had him outnumbered, he was the only immediate threat, and once they had him out of the way they could safely rejoin Provo and get back to Provo's gold. So they had a stake in putting Burgade away, and they hadn't turned back. He'd counted on that.

Gant came by almost near enough to reach out and touch. Burgade kept still. Gant wasn't likely to see him, and Quesada was back there, moving slowly forward, covering Gant. Quesada had a rifle. Burgade let Gant go by. He didn't start breathing again until Gant was ten feet away. The stink of Gant's body lingered in the air, giving away the man's tense emotions in gamy odours.

Burgade felt clammy. The moon was half over west, throwing its pale light down at an angle through the trees. Gant's boots went crunching up the gentle grade towards the bend beyond which the horses were browsing. Quesada came along more slowly, turning his head both ways and poking the air ahead of him with his rifle. Burgade watched him come. Quesada had lost his hat in the confusion; faint light glimmered on the bald peak of his big head, surrounded by its bushy monk's fringe. The big-nosed face swivelled like a pivoted machine. Burgade saw the set of the drawn-back lips the dim shine of Quesada's oddly neat white teeth.

Gant went out of sight in the trees above. Quesada was getting close, now. Burgade had lost all sight and sound of the third man back in the woods, and that alarmed him, but there was nothing for it but to play it out to a finish now. Quesada was seven feet from him, stopping to turn his head around and study the forest. Crouched in brush, Burgade made a slow shift in his grip on the Springfield, locking his fist around the forestock, holding it like a club. His nostrils dilated, his mouth twisted, he watched Quesada move closer.

When Quesada was even with him, not four feet from his face, Burgade swung the rifle.

Quesada heard the noise and began to wheel. The swinging rifle-stock struck him at the base of the skull. He dropped like a stone.

But he wasn't out. His breath raised frightened puffs of leafage from the ground. He was trying to renew his grip on the rifle. Burgade took one pace forward, dropped to one knee, and twisted the rifle away. He heard the brittle snap of Quesada's finger breaking in the grigger-guard. Quesada. half stunned, began to roll his face upwards and fill his chest to shout.

Burgade stamped the Springfield butt plate down. It squashed Quesada's skull like an egg.

He dragged Quesada into the bushes and stepped out immediately on to the track, walking uphill at a slow gait. The third man was out there somewhere; if that man looked this way and saw a figure walking up behind Gant, he'd think it was still Quesada.

He walked around a few bends and saw Gant up ahead Gant had reached the horses. He was standing splayfooted, looking down at the point where Burgade's bootprints disappeared. His back was broad, slightly hunched over.

Burgade lifted the Springfield. He had a brief moment's hesitation about shooting a man in the back. But death was no different because of the direction from which it came. He took aim and placed his shot with care. The Springfield laid its hard echo across the night and Gant reeled forward, spinning, his head turning on bulging neck tendons, his mouth sagging in stupefaction.

Gant pitched to the ground and rolled over. A back shot was always risky: even a .30-06 could deflect off one of the heavy ribs. And Gant had the size and constitution of a truck horse. The bullet had not put him away. He was grievously hurt — he made no move towards his guns, he sat on the ground supported by both arms and hardly moved, nor did he look up towards Burgade.

That third man was out there somewhere, alerted by the shot. Burgade began to turn into the forest. But then he stopped and deliberately shot Gant in the head.

A wounded man might shoot him in the back. A dead man wouldn't. And Gant was one of those who had raped Susan.

The horses went crashing away. Burgade left Gant there asprawl, dead or too close to it to make any difference. He slipped into the woods to his right and began to stalk the third man.

He headed into the general quadrant where the man ought to be. It didn't take long to rouse a response. The man was rattled, and evidently had no rifle; a pistol opened up from a considerable range. Dropping belly-flat, Burgade heard the slugs ricochet off branches and twigs. He saw the thudding muzzle-flames and dragged the Springfield up to his shoulder and fired.

There was a scream of metal on metal. He saw something arc through the air, something that glittered with a dark oily shine. He knew what it was: his shot, by chance, had struck the man's pistol — not unlikely, since the lancing muzzle-flash had been his aiming point.

Burgade rolled swiftly, two times over, and came to rest propped on both elbows, six feet to one side of the point from which he had fired. He didn't want his opponent to do the same thing to him — use his gun-flame for a target. No telling how many guns the man might have on him.

Nothing. The man didn't know where he was; the man wasn't shooting. Patience quickly drained out of Burgade. He could spend forever waiting. He didn't have time — only this one was left, then there'd be nobody behind him when he went for Provo and the rest. He had to take this one out, and he didn't want to spend all night at it. He got up and began to move forward.

He moved bent over double; crept from tree to tree. Steady and slow: there was no margin for carelessness. It took him fifteen minutes to cross the two hundred feet to where the man had stood to shoot at him, and when he got there the man had faded away into the night. All Burgade found was the smashed pistol.

His bullet had crushed the slide. It was a ·45 automatic pistol. No wonder the man hadn't hit him at that range. It was hard to hit anything with an automatic. Especially if you'd spent the past few years in prison where you couldn't keep in practice . . . He jerked himself back: his mind had been drifting. What a hell of a time to wander off into speculations about guns and prisons.

Flat against a tree, he swept the surroundings. The man might be right around here, frozen in ambush. Or the man might have gone after the horses to get away.

Gamble that he made for the horses. Burgade moved out. It was a risk, but everything was. The men had been rousted by the grass fire, they hadn't had time to gather belongings. They'd made their run for it in confusion. It was worth the gamble that the automatic had been the man's only weapon and that now, without a gun, he was on the run. Burgade took a chance and hurried: he wanted to get the man before he got on a horse and rode out of range.

The noise had driven the horses up in the direction of the

mountain passes, but it was doubtful they'd gone very far. Burgade decided to check them out. If he didn't find the missing man he'd give up on him, get aboard one of the horses, and go around after Provo after scooping up the dead men's weapons, Gant's and Quesada's . . .

That's two, he thought savagely. Two stupid mistakes tonight. Of course that was where the man was headed. Not for the horses. But back to the trail — to get Gant's gun, or Quesada's. And by now it was probably too late to stop him.

In a bleak rage, embittered by his own blunders, Burgade wheeled back towards the trail, crowded by urgency. He came swinging past the thick dark bole of pine, and that was when Portugee Shiraz jumped him with a knife.

His sluggish reflexes wouldn't have been enough to save him if he hadn't been moving faster than a man ought to move through dark timber with an enemy nearby. Shiraz plunged out from behind the tree, whipping the knife up in a wicked arc that should have split him from crotch to chest-plate. But Shiraz hadn't expected him to be moving so fast Shiraz had to correct his aim and when Burgade's slow reflexes took effect and began to wheel him to one side, the knife lodged point-first against his breast-bone with Shiraz's dark lean weight behind it.

Burgade was in momentum: his unstoppable forward lunge knocked Shiraz's arm aside. The knife had pricked the skin and scraped the hard bone, that was all, and now he was falling away to the side in unbalanced reaction to the collision.

Shiraz was faster, surer on his feet. He had his balance now and he was closing fast against the threat of the rifle. Shiraz's boot slammed down on top of the rifle, banging Burgade's knuckles against the earth. The knife was whipping forward again but Burgade saw it in time and blocked Shiraz's wrist with his own; locked his fist around the dark forearm and twisted, pulling, using Shiraz's own fast-moving inertia to propel him past. Shiraz went right over him.

Shiraz's boot slipped and turned on the hard surface of the rifle and when Shiraz fell, the rifle skittered away into the brush, propelled by his skidding boot-sole.

Burgade rolled over violently away from Shiraz, and fumbled for his holster.

It was empty.

The revolver had fallen out when he'd rolled over — and Shiraz was coming at him now, no time to hunt for it. He scrabbled away from the attack, getting his feet under him and Shiraz tripped. Shiraz didn't fall, but it gave Burgade time to get on his feet. When Shiraz had finished windmilling his arms for balance and straightened up, Burgade was crouching, facing him, both arms wide, ready for him, watching from the pained depths of his red sleepless eyes.

The air was charged with sudden quiet. Burgade's breathing was tight and shallow, his sphincter contracted, his palms damp.

Shiraz studied him, moving slowly with the knife circling in his outstretched fist, slowly driving Burgade back ahead of it. Shiraz's eye sockets were sunken and charcoal-fiery, emanating hatred. He bit a hangnail on his thumb and knitted the brows of his black vulpine face. 'I'm onna admire to stick this knaff in you, Burgade.'

Burgade didn't waste wind talking. He felt a tree at his shoulderblade: he wheeled, curled behind it, and used that brief moment of respite to whip his jacket off and wrap it around his left forearm in a heavy muff.

Shiraz came prowling past the tree, after him, in no hurry, measuring him. Burgade kept circling. Shiraz moved closer, moving the knife in a little spiral, and then Burgade lunged, swiped his wadded coat at the knife, snagged the blade against the cloth and deflected it, spun half to one side and used his foot — cracked his heavy boot-heel against the front of Shiraz's shin.

It was a hard kick, almost hard enough to break the bone. Shiraz stumbled, withdrawing the knife. Burgade got both hands on the knife arm, bent it back, used his weight to push Shiraz over. They fell into a bush. A branch raked Burgade's cheek, almost got his eye. Gripping the knife wrist, he smelled Shiraz's sour breath and heard gristle snap in his own shoulder; he heard himself gasping.

Shiraz's black face was drawn with pain but he had strength and speed all over Burgade. He wrenched himself aside and broke Burgade's grip and fell off the bush, never losing his grip on the knife handle. The blade ripped away the jacket from Burgade's arm and Shiraz rolled free.

Burgade batted his arms at the bush getting free, ripped his flesh on nettles, spun toward Shiraz and, when the man got his hands down to lift himself off the ground, kicked Shiraz in the face.

Shiraz's head rocked back. Burgade kicked him again. He heard the snap of cartliage in Shiraz's nose; blood sprayed over his boot and Shiraz cried out. Burgade stamped his boot, grinding, until the fingers splayed open. He reached down, scooped up the knife, and plunged it up in a short sweeping arc into Shiraz's exposed belly.

He yanked the knife out and stood wobbling, unable to get breath into his throat.

Shiraz's hands clutched his belly, trying to hold the blood in.

Burgade straightened up very slowly, soaked in his own juices. There was a powerful tremor behind his knees. Vomit pain convulsed his stomach but he stood there motionless and watched Shiraz fall back on to the earth. The hands dropped away and when blood stopped spurting from the long slash he knew the heart had stopped pumping. Shiraz's mouth hung open, the bad teeth exposed, eyes open and staring at the moon.

He made sure Shiraz was dead. He closed the eyelids and went prowling for his guns. Found them, straightened up, and said to himself 'Horse, next.' And then the reaction hit him, a chill, a tremor, a hot flush that prickled his scalp. He closed his eyes and felt a dizzy nausea, bright red flickers on the insides of his eyelids, a trembling faintness against which he locked the muscles of his stomach and pectoris and biceps.

His whole body began to shake. He had to cling to a tree. There was a wave of flaccid weakness, almost unconsciousness. The quaking tremor seized him again, and he had to grip the tree with all his strength.

Finally the spasm passed. His muscles loosened. He gasped for breath, sucking and gulping: he felt very cold.

The horses had gone farther than he had anticipated. Their track was easy enough to follow, even after the moon descended, but he had to stop and rest three times and didn't catch up with them until almost dawn. Then he just sat down near them and let them get used to having him around, smelling him, watching him. He closed his eyes momentarily, his head back against a tree trunk, but jerked them open immediately. He'd almost fallen asleep.

Methodically he filled the magazine of the Springfield from the loose shells in his pocket. He examined his revolver to make sure the fall in the dirt hadn't plugged its muzzle; holstered it snugly and had a very hard time lifting himself to his feet. He staggered toward the horses, talking low in his throat to soothe them, and although a few of them backed away with alarmed rolling eyes, two stayed put, unconcerned, and he got his hand on a trailing leather rein. He gathered the reins over the horse's withers and tried to lift his left foot into the the stirrup but he just didn't have the strength. He closed his eyes and leaned against the saddle, dragging breath into his chest. There was a painful sting where Shiraz's knife-point had dug into his breastplate, but when he touched it with his fingers inside his shirt, he felt the sticky dryness of a forming scab and knew it was all right, it wasn't bleeding. His cheek was hot with pain too — a branch had raked him but that was no more serious than a shaving cut. He was intact, but barely; there was no energy left. Just getting on a horse was beginning to appear beyond his capacities.

Finally he led the horse over to a steeper part of the hillside and manoeuvred it around until its left side was toward the high side of the hill. It was like standing on a box beside the horse — the extra foot of ground elevation was enough for him to get his foot into the stirrup and heave himself on to the seat. He settled himself down firmly in the saddle and gigged the horse gently, and rode down the hill with the first pale streaks of dawn behind him.

They were on foot; it was just about the only advantage he had over them — that and the fact that they must have heard the shooting and might feel half confident that Gant and Quesada and Shiraz had taken care of him. He ticked them off in his mind, those who were left against him: Provo, and Menendez, and the kid Shelby. They still had Susan. Hal was somewhere around, batting around in the hills, but he didn't know whether Hal had waited around after setting the fire to see what happened. Hal might have gone back up the mountain to the stream where Burgade had decided to rendezvous if he'd gotten Susan away from them. If Hal had gone up there he couldn't be expected to get back down here before mid-morning at the earliest. He dismissed Hal from his calculations.

Daylight grew stronger as he rode slowly down through the forest. He followed the same trail the horses had used in going up. Just on sunrise he came across Gant's undisturbed body in the trail. The odor was already heavy, a rancid stench; Gant's color had changed in death.

Fifty yards farther he glanced into the brush and saw Quesada where he had dragged him back off the trail. The formation of gases had bloated the corpse, flies buzzed around his head. Here too was the sweet rotten smell of beginning decay. Insects and carrion would clean up everything but the bones, and as the bones rotted their calcium would help feed the ancient and unchangeable forest. Nature was efficient, nothing went to waste. Efficient and indifferent: the forest would not care whether, in the end, it be Zach Provo's bones or Sam Burgade's that stayed behind to nourish it.

Young Shelby posed a nuisance, merely because he was a third gun to account for, but it was the other two who made it look pretty close to impossible. Provo and Menendez were faster and shrewder and five times as tough as any of the others. Burgade had only vanquished Gant's three because they had been stupid enough to split up. Provo wouldn't make that kind of mistake. Provo would keep close to his comrades and he would keep Susan tight by him as a shield.

But there was nothing else to do but keep taking chances until there were no chances left. Burgade rode straight on down to within twenty yards of the burnt-out meadow. The smell of smoke still hung vaguely in the air, enough to make the horse skittish, but the fire had burned itself out against the damp edge of the woods, and only the trees right along the edge had been scorched. Out there on the flat he could barely make out the scorched remains of Taco Riva's body, where Riva had fallen off his horse with a bullet in his head and the fire had swept right over him. Heat had sucked the yellow fats out of Riva's body and he was a pale unrecognisable mass out there with birds picking at him. Burgade turned left inside the fringe of the trees and began to work his way around towards the far side of the big meadow, where Provo had taken Susan last night. Most likely they weren't still there, but it was the place to start tracking.

CHAPTER ELEVEN

UP here on the heights wind had stunted the trees and made them hunchbacked, and the steep earth was a spindly web of sunlight and shadow. The four of them stopped beside a rock parapet that commanded the western plain from the summit. From this high rim the redrock cliffs, smoothed and sanded by millennia of hard west winds, pitched down a thousand feet, almost vertically, into the dropaway mountains below and the desert plain beyond. The razorback summit was so narrow that from this vantage point Zach Provo could see across the divide in both directions, east and west, without moving his feet the precipice to the west, the steplike tiers of wooded mountians to the east — the way they had just come.

Provo removed his tattered duster. The coat had flowed and flapped, ripped on nettles, hampered him terribly, but he had kept it because its pockets were filled with beef jerky and water flask, spyglass and rifle ammunition. He hadn't salvaged much, there hadn't been time with flames rushing maddeningly into camp, and he'd had his hands full with the girl. Now he took off the coat and threw it on the ground to free his arms and body from its hampering folds.

Menendez, seeing him throw the coat down, gave him a hooded look that indicated Menendez knew what the act meant. It meant this was as far as they were going.

Provo's filthy shirt clung to him like the skin of a prune. In his way he had always been fastidious and the stink of himself offended him.

Chalk that up to Sam Burgade too, he thought, and glanced at Susan. She sat with loosely sprawled legs, rumpled, filthy, and too beaten to care. The wind blew her long hair across her face and she didn't comb it away. There were raw red patches on her face and throat that must have come from Gant's beard, and Shiraz's and Quesada's.

He took note of Menendez's restless eyes combing the timber slopes behind. A few yards away, Mike Shelby sat down slowly, rocking with groggy fatigue. They were all living on their nerves.

Menendez said, 'Let me have that glass, eh?' And put it to his eye and squinted. Following the direction of its aim, Provo saw he was looking down towards the big meadow four thousand feet below and more than four miles east — where they had camped before. It was a flat black waste now, all coals and ashes.

Menendez handed him the glass. That little yellow patch,' he said, 'that most be Taco. I thought I es-seen him go down las' night. Focking bast —'

'He's dead,' Provo said. 'Cussing won't help.' He folded the telescope and put it down: he didn't need it to see the buzzards congregating around the three places on the slopes beyond the meadow. And there was a man on horseback coming up behind them: they had spotted him half an hour ago, a couple of miles below them, patiently tracking. If it was any of their own men he'd be coming along faster. It was Burgade, or Burgade's partner, whoever that was.

Menendez said softly, 'The *viejo* is quite a es-stem-winder, ain't he?' There was admiration in his voice.

Provo stared at him with eyes hard as glass.

Mike Shelby said in a cranky worn-out voice, 'The bastard's like some kind of mirage.' Shelby's trousers were charred. He was whacked-out tired, but Provo could sense the tension in him: Shelby crouched like an exhausted beast still ready to spring.

Menendez moved to a new vantage point, clutching the rifle. It was the only one among them. They all had their handguns, but there was only the one rifle left, and that made it bad.

Shelby lifted his head with an effort. 'Listen, we'll never lose him, he'll chase us clear to Canada.'

'Nobody can chase you if you don't run,' Provo said.

'The hell. You want to stay put and end up like Gant and those others?'

'Nobody's quitting. Not until I get his hide nailed to the barn.'

'Zach, we tried, it was no good. To hell with the old man.'

'I'm paying you to help me kill him.'

'You ain't paid us nothing yet.'

'There's thirty-eight thousand in gold left down there. Right down there within half a mile of where we camped. Three caches, two hundred yards apart. You want it, Mike?'

'It? You mean *all* of it?'

'It's yours to split with Menendez.'

He saw Menendez's face change.

But Shelby said, 'Maybe so. Maybe you can pay for my help, Zach, but you ain't got enough gold to pay for my life.'

Provo said, 'Suit yourself, Mike. But you said it yourself. He'll track you all the way to Canada. You may as well make a stand and help us finish him off here.'

'I never should've trusted you,' Shelby muttered. 'I should've learned a long time ago not to trust anybody.'

'Christ,' Provo said in contempt, 'you're not dead yet.'

'Why don' you two es-shut up?'

Menendez was right. They were reduced to petty bickering. Provo clamped his jaw shut and turned to sweep the canyons behind them.

He stiffened. 'There he is. Menendez!'

'I see him.' Menendez had the rifle up, but he didn't shoot. Down below, the horseman was making a quick dash across an open stretch, moving from right to left. Only a quarter of a mile or so — not much more than four hundred yards, well within maximum rifle range. But Menendez was right not to shoot. At that range it would take Menendez's rifle bullet more than a full second to travel to the target. In a full second a horse would cover thirty feet of ground or more. Shooting downhill was chancy at best; against a narrow target moving sideways it was hopeless. The horseman disappeared into the timber.

Provo's voice grated hoarsely. 'It's Burgade, all right.' He made a quick quarter-turn and pointed with his arm. 'He'll come through that notch. He'll be coming right towards us so it won't matter how fast he's moving. Give me the rifle, Menendez, and get down there in those trees inside of a handgun range of him. We'll crossfire him.'

Menendez tossed him the rifle without objection and vaulted into the trees. He went out of sight into the timber and Provo settled down against a rock, bracing the rifle on the clearing where he knew Burgade would appear if Burgade kept on the boot tracks.

But Burgade didn't show up. An overwhelming anxiety slowly poisoned Provo's patience.

Shelby said, 'He's not that dumb, Zach.'

'Shut up.'

'He won't show himself. You know he won't.'

Provo kept his eyes fixed on the clearing below. 'Listen, you just keep watch on missy and let me handle the old man. He ain't going to get close to us as long as we've got a gun on her. You just think about all that gold down there.'

'Yeah,' Shelby said, but his voice was unsteady.

Provo cocked the rifle and squinted through the shimmer of sunlight. A pulse thudded in his eyes. He curled his hand sensuously around the grip of the rifle, caressed the trigger with his finger. *Come on*, he thought. *Come on, now.* He was going to break Burgade's right shoulder with the first bullet. Then take him apart limb by limb. It was going to take Burgade a long time to die.

CHAPTER TWELVE

The sun flickered through the pines like a moving signal lamp. Burgade reined in. The tracks went on up through the trees, out across a little clearing and up towards the summit not far beyond. Provo had to be forted up somewhere between here and there, trying the same kind of ambush he himself had used last night against Quesada. It had to be that way, because Provo had his back to the cliff that dropped away on the west face of the summits. Somewhere in the next three hundred yards, Provo was waiting.

He had ridden for two hours with his body braced against an expected bullet. Taking a chance. Now the chances were all used up. It was a feeling like ice across the back of his neck. He felt exposed, vulnerable, sitting his saddle alone in the forest breeze. The thin high air was crisp with pine smell. Sleeplessness laid a glaze on his eyes; his lids blinked painfully and slowly.

He dismounted with great care and tied the horse's reins to a low branch. Lifted the Springfield in both hands and began to move away to the right. The pitch was steep but the trees gave better cover here, because the high summit protected them from the winds and they grew taller and thicker. He walked very slowly and without sound, placing each foot with caution. But sweat sluiced down his chest and weakness flowed along his fibres.

He heard the revolver hammer snick.

He lowered himself to the ground — fast, but not so fast as to make noise. His chin lifted and he turned his head slowly, staring past the boles of trees. There was no movement, no sound. He thought perhaps the man out there had heard him but not yet seen him. But there was someone, not far away — upwind, because the sound wouldn't have carried from any other direction.

He stared into the wind. That was uphill, towards the summit. He didn't see anything.

He looked back over his shoulder. He could see the horse, twenty-five or thirty feet below him where he had tethered it. Wherever the man was, he was not in position to see that point on the trail; otherwise he'd have fired when Burgade stopped to dismount.

Burgade clawed an egg-sized stone out of the ground and hitched himself slowly up against the wide trunk of a tree that would conceal him from above. He stood up, close to the trunk, dragging the rifle in his left hand, and turned around with his back to the tree. Hefted the little stone and measured his throw and tossed it, not terribly hard, just enough to arc it through the air.

It thudded against the horse's flank. The horse jumped, scrambled around in a half-circle, tried to break its reins. There was a great deal of noise before the horse settled down again.

Burgade lay down flat again with the rifle against his shoulder, pointing past the pine trunk. His view was restricted by the tree trunks but there was no underbrush to speak of; he could see quite well along the ground, between trees. The steep earth was a mat of brown needles and mossy flat rocks.

A figure flitted from tree to tree, quite a distance above him on the grade. A man in a dirty straw hat. Menendez.

Burgade closed his finger around the trigger and waited. He knew where Menendez was now. Menendez would show himself and when he did, Burgade would shoot. Menendez had gone behind the tree from the right. Burgade sighted to the left of it.

But Menendez reappeared at the right, crouched low and moving fast in a spurt. Burgade shifted the rifle and fired.

Too hasty. A miss. Now Menendez knew he'd been spotted. Burgade scraped the side of his chin against his shoulder, irritable — the gunshot would alert the others.

He moved around behind the pine trunk, shifting his position to conceal himself more completely from Menendez's angle. But Menendez didn't stir, and Burgade felt urgency building pressure inside him.

Menendez was waiting him out. That was no good: the others could be coming in from either side. Burgade got to his feet behind the tree, aimed the Springfield past the side of it and let go three shots at Menendez's position. Without waiting, he dropped the rifle and sprinted uphill to his right, dropping flat after a twelve-foot run.

It was just in time: Menendez's revolver opened up. The rolling echoes of the shots caromed down the hill. A bullet shrieked off the trunk of a pine two feet above him, leaving a white scar. Burgade cocked the forty-five and waited for his breathing to settle down. He wasn't much of a runner anymore. He bunched his legs and made a run for a higher pine.

Bullets snapped at his heels. He dived and skidded on his chest. Slid right past the pine, on the slippery needles, and brought the double-action up in time to get a shot at Menendez before Menendez wheeled behind cover.

He had a feeling he might have scored a hit, but Menendez was still shooting. Burgade huddled tight behind the pine, counting bullets. It was clear enough Menendez had two revolvers on him; and Menendez was wise enough not to empty both of them. He'd be using the intervals to reload spent chambers. Burgade stopped counting, reloaded his own, and decided on a cheap ploy that might work if Menendez was rusty enough. Menendez was a Border tough, as shrewd as they came, but to a man like Menendez 'revolver' meant single-action Frontier model. That was why Menendez carried two: because the single-action was slow to reload. You had to punch out the empties one by one and then reload the chambers one by one.

It was only going to work if Menendez assumed Burgade had the same kind of gun.

Burgade slipped a loaded cartridge out of his belt and held it poised in the fingers of his left hand; turned to study Menendez's position with one eye, gathered his legs, and sprinted for a tree eight feet away, blazing away as he ran.

He fired all six, double-action, blinding-fast. It kept Menendez's head down until the last shot was fired. Burgade reached cover and dropped flat, knowing Menendez had been counting. When he hit the ground he already had the side-swing cylinder open. He punched the pin, scattering all the empties at once, plugged the ready cartridge in and slammed the cylinder shut, turning it to line up the brass rim under the hammer . . .

Menendez charged, shooting with one hand, holding the other revolver in reserve. He was running wide in a half-circle to spiral in. Wide open.

Burgade fired.

The bullet rocked Menendez, as a .45 would, no matter where it hit. Menendez skidded to his knees. A red spot showed up, high on the front of his shirt.

Burgade thumbed another cartridge into the revolver and took deliberate aim. Menendez's legs were scrabbling for toe-holds, he was trying to swim towards cover but his elbows and boots kept slipping. Burgade finished him with a slow-aimed bullet.

He went back down to get his rifle. Untied the horse and led it up through the trees to where Menendez lay dead. He loaded both Menendez's revolvers and rammed them into his waistband, and stood a moment getting his breath.

Menendez's body had cleared itself in the moment of death. There was the stink of human excrement. The straw hat had rolled away a few yards. Burgade picked it up, removed his own hat, and put the straw hat on. He hung his black hat over the saddle horn, and tied the horse up. Then he bent down and tried to pick up the corpse.

Menendez wasn't very big. But the wiry little body was too much for him. The old muscles refused to lift it. Burgade got it propped up, seated, against a tree, but that wasn't enough. He went over to the horse and checked out the saddle, but he'd known full well what was on it, and there was no rope. With a rope he might have hauled the body up by slinging the end of the rope over a tree limb and using his own weight.

He sat down to study it out. His mind was slow and vague; there was a red wash of fatigue over his eyes. His body needed nourishment and sleep.

He sat with his mouth slack, breathing with slow lifts and falls of his shoulders. He was like that when he heard the low cautious clop of hoofs coming up from below.

He got the rifle and walked down through the trees and waited. It might be Hal, it might be a Navajo, it might be just about anybody; it wasn't Provo or any of Provo's people, so he was not determined to shoot at first glimpse, but he kept the rifle aimed anyway, on the spot where the approaching horse would appear in the trees below.

It was Hal.

'I heard the shooting. Are you all right?'

'I haven't been shot, if that's what you mean.'

'You weren't up at the creek so I came back. I saw the tracks coming up this way.'

'Lucky you didn't ride into an ambush.'

'What was that shooting, then?'

'Menendez,' Burgade said. He motioned to Hal to dismount. 'Come on — back this way, they've got the clearing under a gun.'

He walked slowly up through the pines. It was an effort just talking to Hal: he spoke in short bursts, his breath coming thin and fast. 'There's only two of them left now. Provo and the kid. Up there with Susan.'

Hal stared at him. 'What happened to the rest of them?'

'Dead.'

'Sweet Jesus,' Hal said in awe. He caught sight of Menendez; stopped and swallowed.

Burgade said 'Help me get him on his horse.'

'Put my hat on him,' Burgade said.

Hal had to get up on his own horse to reach Menendez's

head. Menendez sat slumped on the saddle, hands tied on to the horn by the ends of the reins.

Burgade pointed along the slope. 'Lead his horse over there with you. Wait on the edge of the trees, don't show yourself. Take a post behind a good big tree and don't stick anything out except one eye and your rifle. Give me fifteen minutes to get up there and then whip this horse up the trail. And then start shooting.'

'Shooting? At what?'

'The rocks below the summit. Don't aim higher, you might hit Provo but then again you might hit Susan with a ricochet. Unless you see a perfect target don't try. Just make noise. It'll rattle them and the noise will help cover my approach. Have you got plenty of ammunition?'

'In my saddlebags.'

'Get it. When you get over there, take off your hat and fill it with loose ammunition and keep it on the ground beside you where you can get at it fast. Keep a steady volley of fire going — use up everything you've got until you get down to the last ten or twelve cartridges. You'll want to save those, you may need them if they cut me down. You understand it all?'

'I ought to be the one to go up there. You're in bad shape.'

'I know the drill — you don't. It comes down to that.'

Hal brooded. 'Christ.'

Burgade turned and got his rifle. 'Better make it twenty minutes,' he said bleakly. 'That's a stiff climb for old bones.'

He had to go through shoulder-high scrub trees; he went on his belly, and halfway to the top he stopped to study the rim. It was a long razorback parapet. Probably not more than a few yards wide at the top, with the cliff dropping away on the far side. There were big boulders scattered around, smoothed by the wind. Only one way to get up there from here without exposing himself to a withering fire from the rim — go along to the left and circle up through the field of boulders. It would be taking a chance they weren't waiting there, rather than on top, but he had a feeling they were all the way up on the summit because it was the only place from which they could see down their own backtrail and shoot at pursuers.

By now they would be getting rattled because Menendez hadn't showed up. They were somewhere along that hundred feet of rimrock, probably looking down the trail, but from here the rocks were in the way, he couldn't see anyone. He took a deep breath and moved forward again; there wasn't much time.

In the boulders a hundred feet below the top, he set the rifle down soundlessly and left it there. From here on he'd be within handgun range and a rifle would be unwieldly. He palmed the double-action in his right hand and made his way forward slowly through the boulders, feeling the dig of Menendez's two six-guns in his waistband. The sun blasted down through the thin afternoon air, striking painful reflections off the rocks. He slipped forward along the high wall of a rock and paused while still behind it, in its thin stripe of shadow. The rim was only sixty or seventy feet above him, up a forty-degree pitch littered with house-size rocks. The passages between them were big enough for locomotives to get through, but there was no way to know what was on the far side without showing himself. He waited, sucking breath silently into his chest with his mouth wide open and gulping.

He heard the sudden rataplan of hoofbeats and a startled voice, not Provo's, shouting:

'Jesus, that looks like Burgade!'

And there was a quick succession of reports, crisp in the thin air. Burgade was already moving. He heard Hal's rifle open up from down below. Bullets cranged and whined off the rocks. He climbed as fast as his halting legs would move him, scrambling through the boulders — up through a notch, on to the redrock rim — and he saw Susan immediately, with Shelby right beside her, shooting downhill at Hal's rifle smoke.

The hard snout of a gunbarrel rammed into Burgade's back.

He froze.

Provo's voice, breathing down his neck, said with savage satisfaction. 'You're holding a bust hand, Sam. You're all through now. Drop the iron.'

Fighting reflexes were not instincts. They were the product of training.

Instinct — self-preservation — dictated obeisance. Provo had a gun in his back. Provo didn't intend killing him on the spot; if he'd meant to do that he'd have fired already, without giving warning. No. Provo wanted him to suffer. To die slowly and know what was happening to him.

Shelby had turned his gun toward Susan, not to kill her but to add weight to Provo's threat.

Burgade's gun was already aimed at Shelby. In the split instant of time when Provo quit talking — when Provo was convinced he had his man cold — Burgade fired.

It cost no time to shoot the man he was already aiming at. His bullet hit Shelby dead-centre.

But Burgade wasn't watching. In the instant of pulling trigger he rammed back, twisting, elbowing Provo's gun aside.

He was old. Too slow to get away clear with a trick that would have worked perfectly thirty years ago. Provo's bullet exploded into his body. It propelled him bodily forward with its tremendous muzzle energy.

He hit the ground rolling. Flame streaked out of Provo's gunbarrel. It caught Burgade in mid-turn, smashed his left arm useless, but Burgade had only one purpose in the world and Provo had made the mistake of shooting to cripple, not to kill, and now Burgade completed his falling roll and fired up from the ground, one shot with fifty years of gun training behind it, and it hit Zach Provo in the right eye. It drilled the eye socket empty, sprayed splintered bone fragments from his face. The hole filled with a bursting yellow and crimson pulp and Provo pitched backwards over the rim.

Silence fell. Burgade rolled over. Susan was sitting there beside Shelby's corpse. She didn't move. She didn't seem to recognise him, but she was staring at him. He moved again, felt and heard the broken ends of his bones grate together. Blood pulsed below his rib and a bone showed white. He dragged himself towards Susan. Made it to her and lay there, weak and bleeding. He reached up for her hand and clasped it, and the world went black.

A voice nearby, talking, not making sense. He listened to it but it faded in and out of his hearing. He tried to keep it, but it drifted away and he lost it, and fell away from reality again.

He had a feeling time was passing, a lot of time. A faint sense that someone was touching him, doing something to him. Water in his mouth — someone trying to make him drink. He felt a distant irritation: he wanted to be left alone. Sleep.

His eyes opened. The sky was plum-coloured. Dusk. Or predawn. He was on his back, a cool wind rushed over him, whipping his white hair across his eyes. He seemed to be wrapped in tight bandaging and blankets and clothing, like a sarcophagus. He began to sort out pain, to locate the sources of agony: his arm, his left side. He couldn't feel the fingers of his left hand at all.

He turned his head. The voice was talking again, the same soothing quiet run of talk, just one voice, a man's, very steady and low, talking the sort of comforting nonsense you would talk to a skittish horse. *There, there, now, darling, it's ended, it's over, you're all right, nothing's ever going to hurt you again . . .*

He couldn't see the speaker. He tried to lift his head to look. He got his head an inch off the ground and dizziness overcame him. His eyelids rolled down and he fell back into darkness.

Daylight was red against his eyelids. He squinted irritably. It didn't go away. He opened his eyes and saw the sky, fleece clouds scattered across the cobalt vastness. He turned his head.

Hal said, 'He's awake.'

Burgade spoke. 'Susan.' His voice was a croak.

'She's all right, sir. She's fine. She's right here.'

Hal slipped fingers under his head and lifted him up so he could see.

Susan sat crosslegged on the ground. Both hands were pressed to her temples, her face was preternaturally white, but she was looking at him and she made a tiny, jerky smile that came and went so quickly he wasn't sure if he'd imagined it.

Hal said, 'Here. Drink.'

The canteen touched his mouth and he sucked on it greedily. He lay back and groaned.

Hal said, 'You've got a busted arm and a busted rib. But you're going to be all right. We'll just wait here until you're mended enough to go down.'

'Weed.' Burgade said suddenly.

'I know. I'll go down and bring him up later today, when you're a little better.'

Eight of them, Burgade thought, *and I killed seven.* He felt sick but he held it down.

Wind moaned across the rim. Burgade heard halting little footsteps and when he turned his face he saw Susan getting down on her knees beside him. She reached out with both hands and cupped the sides of his face. Her eyes were very wide and glistening. He saw the tears crawl down her cheeks.

Susan removed one hand from his face and reached for Hal's hand and drew him down beside her. Hal smiled at her and she sat there with one hand on each of them and cried it all out. Afterwards Hal lifted her to her feet and held her in his arms, and Sam Burgade smiled at the sky.

THE THREEPERSONS HUNT

BRIAN GARFIELD

The White Mountain Apache Reservation encompassed two million acres of crumbling foothills and deep, dark forested high country. A dramatic land steeped in the history of a proud race — but now a backcloth to a strange and deadly manhunt.

And Joe Threepersons had to be found. The high-powered .375 magnum rifle that he carried was one reason, a bizarre murder puzzle that he held the answer to was the other. Reasons enough for the Arizona Highway Patrol to send state trooper Sam Watchman into the hunt — a Navajo on the trail of an Apache.

CORONET BOOKS

TRIPWIRE

BRIAN GARFIELD

When you happen to be a soldier without a battle to fight and you're black into the bargain, there's not a lot of honest work to be done. So Boag found himself stealing miner's gold for 'Pickett's Marauders', a wild-looking army of insane killers and learnt — the painful way — that there's no luck that time. A bullet hole had left daylight through his leg instead of through his head. He had nearly suffocated in the Colorado River mud. That would have spelt 'the end' to most sensible men. But Boag was sore and black and mad. He'd busted enough Indians to feel he understood the maxim 'shoot to kill'. He'd been left alive and so long as he stayed in that condition Pickett was going to rue the day he hadn't nailed Boag's black hide to the bottom of the river.

CORONET BOOKS

ADVENTURE AND SUSPENSE FROM CORONET

BRIAN GARFIELD

☐	20139 8	The Threepersons Hunt	50p
☐	20149 5	Tripwire	60p
☐	17873 6	Deep Cover	50p
☐	16786 6	Death Wish	40p
☐	20304 8	What of Terry Conniston?	70p

JOHN GODEY

☐	18772 7	The Taking of Pelham 1 2 3	50p
☐	20006 5	The Clay Assassin	60p
☐	20887 2	The Gun and Mr. Smith	80p
☐	18804 9	The Three Worlds of Johnny Handsome	40p

All these books are available at your local bookshop or newsagent, or can be ordered direct from the publisher. Just tick the titles you want and fill in the form below.

Prices and availability subject to change without notice.

CORONET BOOKS, P.O. Box 11, Falmouth, Cornwall.

Please send cheque or postal order, and allow the following for postage and packing:

U.K. — One book 18p plus 8p per copy for each additional book ordered, up to a maximum of 66p.

B.F.P.O. and EIRE — 18p for the first book plus 8p per copy for the next 6 books, thereafter 3p per book.

OTHER OVERSEAS CUSTOMERS — 20p for the first book and 10p per copy for each additional book.

Name ....

Address ....

....